SAVING SHELBY

PJ FIALA

D1379761

RT
ROLLING
THUNDER

COPYRIGHT

Printed in the United States of America

First published 2021

Fiala, PJ

SAVING SHELBY / PJ Fiala

p. cm.

1. Romance—Fiction. 2. Romance—Suspense. 3. Romance - Military

I. Title – SAVING SHELBY

ISBN: 978-1-942618-58-4

DEDICATION

I've had so many wonderful people come into my life and I want you all to know how much I appreciate it. From each and every reader who takes the time out of their days to read my stories and leave reviews, thank you.
My beautiful, smart and fun Road Queens, who play games with me, post fun memes, keep the conversation rolling and help me create these captivating characters, places, businesses and more. Thank you ladies for your ideas, support and love. The following characters and places were created by:
Diego Josephs - Theresa Sollecito Natole
Diego's dog - Teddy - Jessi Venderveen
Shelby Davidson - Elizabeth Gregory & Jo West Davidson
Shelby's description - Karen Cranford LeBeau
Callie Kennedy - Ginna Honeycutt
Anders Kennedy - Nancy Hoch
Shelby's Niece and Nephew descriptions - Karen Cranford LeBeau
Stacy Kennedy - Doni Turiace
Kurtis Kennedy - Terry Kemmitz & Lisa Rolape Courter

RAPTOR Cook - Sheldon - Marie Evans
RAPTOR Housekeeper - Shioban - Patricia Case
Crest Hills - Christy Seiple
Grasshopper Grove - Lisa Rolape Courter
Fallsville, KC - Patricia Case
SmartTech - Karen Cranford LeBeau
Spencer Wingert - Kristi Hombs Kopydlowski

Special thank yous to the folks who help me along the way and made the production of this book come together.
Thank you to,
April Bennett, my amazing editor.
Stacy Garcia for the fantastic cover.
Eric McKinney of 612 Photography for the photograph on the cover of JD.
Of course, JD - you made this cover!
Julie Collier - without you this all would have been so much harder. Thank you for keeping all the balls in the air!
Judy Wagner - thank you very much for your advice.

Last but not least, my family for the love and sacrifices they have made and continue to make to help me achieve this dream, especially my husband and best friend, Gene.
Words can never express how much you mean to me.
To our veterans and current serving members of our armed forces, police and fire departments, thank you ladies and gentlemen for your hard work and sacrifices; it's with gratitude and thankfulness that I mention you in this forward.

BLURB

R ead the prequel to RAPTOR - RAPTOR Rising here. https://www.pjfiala.com/books/RR-BF

A special operative with a bleeding heart for the innocent.

A desperate kidnapper determined to save the day.

And the desire that explodes between them....

Retraining as an operative in RAPTOR, Diego Josephs is determined to prove himself as a RAPTOR--ready to take down a ruthless kidnapper on the run. But when he encounters the woman who took two children after murdering their mother, everything changes. Nothing is as it seems.

Hellbent on saving her niece and nephew, Shelby Davidson will stop at nothing to reveal the truth about her sinister brother-in-law. She knows in her gut that he had everything to do with her sister's disappearance. But convincing the rugged and irresistible special operative may be harder than she realized. Once Diego relents and realizes she's telling the truth, he knows one thing is certain: he must protect the children while saving Shelby.

***

Read the prequel to the RAPTOR Series, RAPTOR Rising here: https://www.pjfiala.com/books/RR-BF

Let's stay in contact, join my newsletter so I can let you know about new releases, sales, promotions and more. https://www.subscribepage.com/pjfialafm

GLOSSARY

Read the prequel to RAPTOR - RAPTOR Rising here. https://www.pjfiala.com/books/RR-BF

A Note from Emersyn Copeland:

Founder of RAPTOR (Revenge And Protect Team Operation Recovery).

I was wounded when my convoy hit an IED and retrained through OLA (Operation Live Again) to perform useful services for the military; mainly locating missing children. Empowered by the work but frustrated by governmental limitations, I contacted my father Dane Copeland and my Uncle Gaige Vickers, GHOST's leader, to form a covert group not restricted by governmental regulations, consisting of highly trained post military men and women with injuries and disabilities. Our offices are housed on the GHOST compound. I divided RAPTOR into three teams of expertly trained individuals who were selected for their specific abilities. Let me introduce you to the Teams.

Team Alpha: Recon and Recovery:

Diego Josephs: Former Army Recon expert. Friend of GHOST Josh Masters. Recent retraining for OLR (Operation Live Again). Demonstrative and possessive, he is a team player battling PTSD.

Ted: Diego's Therapy and service dog. A mix of black lab and Newfoundland.

Donovan "Van" Keach aka the "Reformer": Completed OLR with Emersyn. Blinded in his left eye during a military operation. Out spoken, opinionated, daredevil with a strong belief in service and a mission for justice no matter the risk.

Charlesia "Charly" Sampson: A friend of Emersyn's Aunt Sophie. Medically discharged after she lost her left arm at the elbow during a mission in Afghanistan. Tough adaptable, independent sarcastic, and determined but self-conscious of her appearance. Excels in disarming and getting people to trust her and ferreting out information.

Team Bravo: Cyber Intelligence:

Piper Dillon: Attractive and energetic with a ready smile but all business. Expert computer hacker, communications device expert and internet guru.

Caiden Marx: Strong and independent, Caiden suffered lung damage while serving due to an explosion and fire. He struggles to breathe and can't take on energetic tasks but excels on Team Bravo and has unique hacker abilities.

Deacon Smythe: Deacon has a ready smile and is always happy but takes his job seriously. He's an expert on computers and communications.

Team Charlie, Special Ops:

Falcon Montgomery: Son of Ford Montgomery, a GHOST team member, Falcon lost hearing in his right ear. Growing up with Ford, Falcon is a natural in special ops, and willing to go the extra mile to get the job done.

Creed Rowan: Former SEAL, well rounded in terms of skill, Creed's specialties are explosives and swimming. His abilities take him places others don't dare go.

Emersyn Copeland: Daughter of GHOST founder, Dane Copeland and niece to current GHOST owner, Gaige Vickers, Emersyn's strengths are in business and extracting her staff member's special talents. But, she's equally good at ferreting out suspects' deep dark secrets.

House Staff:

Sheldon Daniels, Cook: Former military, Marine. Friend of GHOST's house keeper and cook Mrs. James. Demands order in his kitchen, punctuality and the keeper of all secrets, bonus he's a damned good cook.

Shioban O'Hearn, Housekeeper: Sassy mid- thirties housekeeper. Loves the thrill of working with badasses, but doesn't let herself get walked on.

1

———

Shelby picked up the suitcase she'd packed for her niece, Callie, and her nephew, Anders. She'd babysat for them today, something she did at least once a week, but today she came knowing things were going to change.

Hauling the luggage down the grand staircase, as her sister had lovingly dubbed it, she held tight to the banister, knowing every second counted. Her brother-in-law, Kurtis, had left twenty minutes ago and she only had three hours to get as far away from here as possible.

Setting the heavy suitcase on the floor at the bottom of the stairs, she pulled up the handle and quickly walked to the living room where the kids were watching a cartoon movie.

"Okay kiddos, let's get rolling."

Callie turned to her, a slight pout on her lips. "But Aunt Shelby, we love this movie."

Smiling at her beautiful niece, her curly dark hair pushed back with a pink headband, she said, "I know you do and I have a surprise for you. You can watch it in my car."

Anders jumped up. "Yay!"

Anders and Callie were only two years apart, Callie seven and Anders five, but both of them were mature beyond their years. They'd had to grow up fast in the past month.

"Okay, turn the television off. I have this movie in the car and ready to go for you. And I have snacks."

Callie grabbed the remote and pointed it at the television, promptly turning it off. She then walked to the table alongside the sofa, opened the drawer and neatly set the remote inside. Their father didn't allow anything out of place.

Callie grabbed Anders' hand and they followed her to the door that led to the garage, where they'd get in the vehicle without anyone seeing a suitcase being tucked in the back.

Shelby opened the back door of the SUV, her precious Explorer that she'd scrimped and saved for, and the kids scrambled in.

Shelby leaned in and buckled Anders in, then walked to the other side and double-checked Callie's seat belt. Opening the hatch, she hefted the suitcase into the back, then tugged the large cooler she'd packed at home toward her. Pulling out two juice bottles and two homemade egg, bacon and cheese breakfast muffins, she took great care to set each one of them up with their snacks.

Shelby hopped into the driver's seat, turned on the DVD player and pushed the buttons to start their favorite movie playing. Taking a deep breath and sending up a silent prayer that she'd get them out of the state in time, she tapped the garage door opener and put the Explorer in reverse.

A quick glance at the clock told her she now had two hours and fifteen minutes to make tracks.

She figured that with stops they'd be in Indiana in about five hours. She knew the kids would need a break, but she hoped to keep it to a minimum. She'd keep her phone on until her brother-in-law called to check in, then she'd turn it off so he'd not be any the wiser. Hopefully.

She didn't want to alert the controlling bastard that she'd taken the kids any sooner than necessary.

This plan had to work. She couldn't lose these kids too. Bad enough that she suspected Kurtis had killed her sister —or at a minimum, had her killed. Stacy would never have up and left her kids. She'd never leave them alone with that bastard. Something was sinister about him and the second she'd overheard him on the phone yesterday telling someone he had to "deal with Stacy's brats," she feared they'd soon turn up missing, too. That would be like death to her. These two little loves were all she had of her sister. She'd keep them safe, no matter what she had to do.

When Shelby's phone rang, she jumped, tapped the button to turn off her Bluetooth, and put it to her ear.

"Hello."

"It's me. Everything all right?"

"Yes, everything is wonderful. They're watching a movie right now."

"Don't let them sit there all day watching that mindless crap on the television. They're spoiled as it is, thanks in large part to you."

"It's my pleasure."

His growl on the other end of the phone was an indicator of his mood. She inhaled slowly and exhaled the same.

"Make sure they get outside today."

"Will do. I thought we'd go for a walk in a bit."

He practically growled again. "Tire them out so I don't have to deal with whining and crying when I get home."

"I will."

The line went dead and she turned her phone off, careful to watch the road. She tossed it on the seat next to her.

"Daddy's mad." Callie said.

"No, honey. He just wants to make sure you get some fresh air." She lied.

Shelby looked into the mirror at Callie's sweet face. Poor baby was biting her bottom lip, she was so nervous about her father.

"It's okay honey, we'll get some fresh air on our adventure."

Shelby's eyes darted to Anders whose blue eyes were large and round as he assessed the mood in the car.

She smiled at him. "Okay kids, I have a surprise. We're going on a road trip. We'll be in the car for a while today, so sit back and watch your movie and I'll go as fast as is safe so we can get there sooner."

"Where're we going?"

She was waiting for that question. "I thought maybe we'd go see a big zoo. Would you like that?"

Anders clapped his hands. "I wanna see monkeys!"

Callie smiled. "I want to see the lions."

Shelby nodded and quickly glanced up at each of them in the mirror.

They drove a few miles and Callie softly asked, "Is Daddy going to be mad?"

Shelby shook her head. "I'll take care of it. We'll be gone a few days so he'll have time to settle."

Anders giggled. "We're spending the night?"

"You bet, buddy."

If Shelby had her way about it, they'd spend the rest of their lives without that asshole and she was doing the best she could to ensure that.

Diego stepped from the shower, which was wonderful after a full-fledged, hot sweaty workout, and toweled himself off. Looking around his bathroom, which he was still getting used to, he chuckled.

He'd started working for RAPTOR just over a year ago, and in the beginning they lived out of hotels nearby their newly constructed compound. The GHOST facility was next door, which is where they worked out. They also used the GHOST gun range. It all reminded him of an upscale version of being in the military. Men and women, all of like minds, all working in dangerous jobs, all loving what they did, at every turn. But, unlike the military, they could come back home to their own apartments within the compound, which was built with an old southern mansion facade. Unlike the GHOST mansion next door, which was a converted mansion.

Emersyn Copeland was no dummy, that's for sure. She put pencil to paper and learned that she could build a structure, just as they needed it, then put a facade on the outside of it to blend in with the neighborhood without the expense of retrofitting an existing building.

They had small apartments here, minus the kitchen. They had a main kitchen area and they'd recently hired a cook and a housekeeper. The first thing Emersyn did was ask Ms. James, the GHOST cook and, basically, manager of the facility, to help her interview cooks and housekeepers. Since the nature of their jobs was often covert, always dangerous and confidentiality was a must, the perfect match was important. Turned out, Ms. James had a friend she highly recommended and the two of them worked closely with each other. Ms. James had trained their new cook, Sheldon. Former military, he could still kick some ass, which was noted when Diego walked in on Sheldon working out, and he understood confidentiality.

Their housekeeper, Shioban, was mid-to-late thirties and she had a touch of sass in her. But she did a great job and had the ability to just disappear into the room. The house always smelled of fresh baked bread and gourmet food. It would be difficult not to gain weight working here. Sheldon assured them his food was lower in calories, but it was damned delicious and hard to believe.

His apartment consisted of a living room area, his bedroom complete with walk-in closet, and his bathroom. All of the apartments were the same, and Emersyn had told them to decorate however they chose. He hadn't done anything yet. It wasn't his cup of tea. So his walls were still a very nice tan, his carpeting the same, and he was fine with that. Eventually, he'd hang a picture or two.

Walking to his closet, he stepped inside and dressed. It was the usual for him, black tactical pants and a black moisture-wicking long-sleeved shirt. No fuss. No muss.

Strapping on his gun, pocketing his wallet and his phone, he felt a vibration the second his hand slipped from his pocket.

Pulling the phone free, he saw Emersyn's name on the read-out.

"Josephs."

"Hey Diego, I just got a call on two missing children, ages seven and five. Brother and sister. Believed kidnapper is their aunt, Shelby Davidson. Can you take lead on this one?"

"Yeah. I'll be right down."

"Sounds good. I'll have the report file ready for you."

He hung up, pocketed his phone again, laced up his boots and whistled for his dog, Teddy, a mix of black lab and Newfoundland, who slept peacefully in the corner on his bed. As soon as he heard Diego whistle, he jumped up and walked to his master. Diego pulled Ted's red working vest off the hook next to the door and the second the last buckle was clicked, Ted began whining and shaking. He was going to work and he loved it.

They left his apartment on the second floor. There were ten apartments in the building in all, five on the second floor, five on the main level. Their operations were underground, like GHOST. Their garage, however, unlike GHOST, was at the back of the building and completely enclosed.

He waved his key card in front of the elevator panel on the wall and the door silently whispered open.

Stepping inside, Ted sat, dutifully staring up at Diego, waiting for a command. He was a fantastic dog. Diego needed Ted, his therapy dog had been the main reason Diego's recovery had progressed so quickly. When he had a panic attack brought on by his PTSD, Ted sensed it and laid his chin on Diego's lap or pushed his body against Diego to comfort him.

The doors slid open in the lower level and he and Ted walked to the computer command center. The Cyber Intelligence team, TEAM BRAVO, were amazing on those computers. They did go out in the field sometimes, though usually you could find them in front of their computers, ferreting out pedophiles, criminals, hackers and the like.

He opened the frosted glass door to the Command room and the activity was invigorating. His heart beat faster; excitement to get on the job once again after a couple of days off wove itself through his body. Even Ted was ready to go.

"Ah, Diego." Emersyn pulled a file from the desk where she sat.

"So, we're investigating our client to make sure he's legit, but in the meantime here's what we have from him."

Emersyn limped to the conference table that divided the room, the Cyber Intel group to the left, the rest of the teams' desks to the right. Emersyn's desk, when she wasn't in the field, was directly across the room from the door.

She opened the file to pictures of the brother and sister, both of them dark haired with light blue eyes, both smiling, adorable children. On the opposite page was the picture of their Aunt Shelby Davidson, who looked similar to the children, except her eyes were the prettiest green he'd ever seen. Light green irises with a dark green ring around the outside. With her long dark hair, her eyes looked even lighter.

"These are the children, Callie Kennedy, age seven and Anders Kennedy, age five. Their mother went missing about a month ago, no luck in finding her yet. Their father, Kurtis Kennedy, claims Shelby is unable to have her own children and took an overly possessive interest in her sister, Stacy, the mother, and the children when they were born. She babysat regularly for them while Kurtis had to go to work. He owns a tech company, SmartTech. He came home today to find them gone and Shelby isn't answering her phone."

"What if they're in trouble and not kidnapped?"

"We're looking into that too. Piper is looking into accident reports, car jackings, and cameras in and around the area to see if they can ensure they weren't in an accident. Kurtis doesn't believe so. Also, he's a rather terse individual to deal with, so there's that."

"Okay, so last knowns?" Diego stared at the pictures of the three; anyone seeing them would naturally assume Shelby was their mother. Her long dark hair curled gently over her shoulder in the photograph, just as Callie's did.

"They were at the Kennedy home when Mr. Kennedy left for work this morning. No plans to go out."

"Okay. So last time he saw the children was when?"

"Nine this morning."

Diego looked at his watch, it was now six p.m. Nine hours.

"Why did he wait so long to call?"

"I guess he called Shelby at nine forty-five this morning to check in like he always does. She was fine, the kids were watching a movie when he left for work. He tried calling again at ten thirty and there was no answer. He got busy and didn't get home until around one p.m. They weren't around. Shelby isn't answering her phone. He claims he waited and tried calling her and when he didn't get an answer, he went out looking at some of the kids' favorite places."

"Okay. Does he have security cameras?"

"Yes, he's sending us the footage via our secured file share. I'll upload it when I get it. He lives outside of Kansas City. He called us because we were recommended by a friend of his who set up his security cameras. Word's getting out."

Diego smiled. "That's great."

Emersyn smiled, closed the file and handed it to him. "It is. Soon we'll be able to buy some of that cool equipment GHOST has rather than borrowing it."

Diego picked up the file and started toward the door, Ted dutifully at his side.

3

Shelby turned her SUV right, off the road and onto the dirt driveway of the trailer she'd just rented. The drive was steep, down toward the woods and a sharp left before the trailer came into view from this direction. It sure didn't look like the picture she'd found, but the owner had let her pay cash, didn't ask any questions and assured her it was safe, so it was home for a day or two until she could figure out what to do next.

"Is that where we're staying?" Callie asked.

Shelby twisted in her seat and looked at Callie. "You bet. Shall we go and take a look at the inside?"

"I don't know. It looks gross."

Shelby laughed. This girl was growing up way too fast. "Well, let's not judge until we see the inside. This is our big adventure week. Let's go adventure. Look at these woods. We'll go find some nuts and fun leaves to color and all kinds of fun things when we go exploring tomorrow."

Callie looked out her window at the woods and smiled. "Okay."

Shelby stepped out of her side of the vehicle and opened the back door, unbuckling Anders from his car seat.

"You both did so good today. When we stopped for groceries, I bought some treats just because you were extra special good."

Anders clapped his hands. "What did you get?"

"Ice cream." She smiled at the look of delight on his face and Callie laughed.

"Chocolate?"

"Yes."

"Yay."

Callie unbuckled her seatbelt and stood on the floor between the seats. At seven, her petite frame and height allowed her to tuck into many places most couldn't at her age. Anders was already beginning to sprout and stretch. He'd likely be tall like his father.

Lifting Anders down from the vehicle first, she then reached in and lifted Callie out. Once both were on the ground, she walked to the back of the vehicle, sent up a silent prayer that this place wouldn't be bad inside and opened the hatch. Pulling suitcases from the back, she walked around to the front door of the trailer and took a deep breath. They walked up the three steps to the door, she pulled the keys from her purse and unlocked it.

First glance had her feeling better. The inside wasn't bad. The furniture was well used but well kept, the place smelled clean and fresh. She flipped the light switch on and it immediately brightened the place. Anders stepped into the living room and saw the game console and immediately laughed.

"Callie they have games."

Callie walked in, her initial reticence slowly slipping away. She looked at the game console then to Shelby.

"Can we play?"

"Sure, why don't you two play a few games and I'll get the groceries and other suitcase out of the vehicle."

The kids began turning things on and Shelby investigated the trailer a bit further. The wooden table and chairs in the kitchen were clean and matching and looked sturdy. The counters were clear of clutter, neat and clean. She felt better by the minute.

She then walked through the living room to the back of the trailer to see the bathroom and bedrooms. There were two bedrooms, one bathroom and it was neat as well. All blue and dated, but clean. The two bedrooms were both fitted with bunk beds. The bottom a double size the top a twin. If the kids were uncomfortable sleeping alone in their room, she'd sleep with Callie on the bottom and Anders could sleep on top. They'd make this work.

She looked at the clock on the wall and wondered what was happening back home. By now, Kurtis would be screaming up a storm and stomping through the house and her heart hammered at the thought. But she just knew he'd done something to her sister. She and Stacy talked about everything and Stacy mentioned often about how abusive he was. The last couple of months Stacy had gone so far as to say, "If anything ever happens to me, protect my babies." That was too much of a coincidence to make her comfortable.

On top of that, it was weird that police just shrugged their shoulders and did very little to find Stacy. Kurtis had them believing Stacy went off on her own. There had been a couple of charges on her credit card after she disappeared, from Colorado. When she asked the investigating officer if they were looking into it, she basically told her not to worry about it, things were under control.

Back in the living room, she smiled that the kids were engrossed in their game and she was grateful they had something to enjoy after their long day in the car.

"I'll be right back in kids."

Neither one replied to her so she walked outside and to the SUV. Pulling a couple bags of groceries from the back, she carried them in and set them just inside the door. Turning to grab the last of their things, she decided to turn her SUV around in case she needed to make a quick getaway. The longer time went on, the more she regretted how she handled this, but how could she fight Kurtis? He had money, loads of it. He had a hold on the police it seemed, and after she'd heard him calling the kids, his kids, Stacy's brats and not wanting anything to do with them, she just knew he'd done something to Stacy and he'd also harm the kids.

If Stacy was still alive, she'd get in contact with her, she knew she would. It was unlikely that he was holding her hostage somewhere, that would make no sense. She was more convinced by the day, and by his lack of interest in locating her and the fact that he calmly went about his business as if she'd never existed, that he killed her or had her killed. That was more likely. Kurtis would be careful to not get his own hands dirty. Though having someone killed was just as dirty as killing someone. Maybe even scarier, because it proved he had no qualms about getting people out of the way.

4

D iego stopped behind Piper on his way to the door. "Hey Pipes, you'll send me anything you find?"

She nodded her head without looking away from her screen. "You know I will, Diego."

With her short blond hair and bright blue eyes, Piper was an attractive, energetic woman. She always had a smile on her face, and she was always business first.

Ted followed Diego out the door, his tail eagerly wagging. "Gotta go get our gear bud."

Ted sat next to Diego as if he somehow understood there would be a delay in getting to work. Waving his key card in front of the panel, the elevator doors opened and they both stepped inside.

Pressing the "2" Diego heard his phone chime and pulled his phone up. Piper had sent him the file. The text said, "All uploaded."

Shaking his head, he pocketed his phone as the doors opened once again. He and Ted stepped out of the elevator and turned right. Waving his card in front of the panel, his apartment door unlocked. He walked straight to the closet and pulled out his go bag and began packing extra clothes inside. Just as Ms. James, the GHOST housekeeper/cook taught him, Sheldon had all the little packs of coffees and meal bars in the kitchen in baskets for them each. Shioban was tasked with setting up the shaving packs.

"Okay Ted, let's go to the kitchen and get food to take with us."

Now Ted became excited again, it was time to work.

They made their way to the kitchen on the first floor, and he pulled some coffee packs from the cupboard then walked to the end of the kitchen and pulled some prepackaged food packs for Ted. Grabbing a gallon of water from the refrigerator for Ted, he turned to leave just as Sheldon walked into the kitchen.

"You off then?" He asked in his gruff, raspy voice.

"Yep. Thanks for having the food packs ready. They sure do help."

"My pleasure."

Sheldon leaned down and patted Ted's head, then scratched him behind the ears. Usually when Ted was working, no one touched him, he was on duty. But, Ted took to Sheldon for some reason. Could be that he smelled like food and Ted loved to eat. But, Sheldon was no nonsense and matter of fact and Ted seemed to sense that too. After a couple pats and a scratch, they both left each other alone and both of them seemed fine with that.

"See you in a couple of days Shel."

"Keep your head down."

As he walked out of the kitchen, Diego could hear Sheldon whistling and he smiled.

Walking out the side door, just to the right of the kitchen, Diego grabbed Ted's leash from the hook and they exited into the garage.

He opened his back driver's side truck door, and Ted jumped in. Diego then opened the lid of the small, electric cooler he had on the floor, plugged it into his truck outlet, set the gallon water jug inside to keep it cool for Ted, dropped Ted's leash on the floor alongside the cooler and patted his best friend on the head.

Closing the door and climbing in behind the driver's seat, Diego started his truck up, and slowly drove toward the door, tapping the button to open it on his visor.

The garage filled with light as the door opened and Diego slowly exited the building. As the garage door closed, he set his phone in the holder on the dash, pulled up the coordinates that Piper had sent him and he drove from the compound and toward his destination of where Shelby had last been seen with the kids.

5

———

Shelby looked at the time on the burner phone she'd purchased and realized it was time to get the kids baths and then off to bed. Tomorrow, they'd go out in the woods and do some exploring and hopefully the kids would be tired out in the evening. So far, they'd asked very few questions and actually had begun to relax a bit now that their father wasn't skulking around and being his general verbally abusive self.

"Okay kids, let's go get into the bath and put pajamas on. Then, I'll make some popcorn before we go to bed. Deal?"

Anders turned and looked at her. "Can I finish my game?"

"I'll give you five more minutes, then we need to shut it off. Okay?"

"Okay. This one isn't connected like my regular game."

"What do you mean?"

"You know, the internet."

"Oh, I'm sorry. Maybe our next stop will have internet for you."

Callie headed to the bathroom and Shelby walked in behind her. "Did you want to take a bath by yourself tonight Callie?"

"Yeah." She seemed tired.

Shelby sat on the closed toilet lid and pulled Callie into her arms.

"Is everything alright?"

Callie only nodded and Shelby continued to hold her close.

"I miss your momma so much Callie girl, I'm sure you do too."

She sniffed and Shelby blinked rapidly to dry the tears forming in her eyes.

"I don't think Daddy wants us anymore. He's been mean."

Shelby's heart began to race but she didn't want to overreact. "In what way honey?"

Callie shrugged. "He says we're bad. He's sorry he has to deal with us."

"Oh, honey, I'll bet he doesn't mean that, he's just worried." Shelby hugged Callie tighter. "But, you know what?" She pulled back just a bit. "I don't think you're bad. You are the best little lady I've ever seen and remember, I work in a daycare. And, I'm so happy when I'm with you and Anders. So happy."

Callie only nodded and Shelby's heart hurt for this little girl. Where she'd wavered earlier thinking maybe she'd been a bit impulsive to take the kids and run, she now realized it was the best thing to do. Kurtis was obviously not treating them well.

"Okay, let's get a bath started for you. I have your pink bunny pajamas and your yellow and white striped pajamas. Which ones do you want to wear?"

"Yellow."

"You got it."

Shelby squeezed her niece once more before turning the water on in the bathtub. Shelby had stashed their suitcases in the bedroom to the left of the bathroom. She pulled Callie's pjs and some clean underwear from the suitcase and a pair of Anders' jammies and clean underwear from his suitcase, then walked back into the bathroom.

She set the clothes on the counter; Callie was still standing next to the tub and staring at the water.

"Hey baby, go ahead and get undressed, okay?"

Callie nodded and Shelby stepped out quickly to check on Anders. "Hey buddy, time's up."

"Okay." Anders said rather sadly.

She knew from experience that he wouldn't stop right away and she figured that would give Callie time to bathe. She then went into the bathroom to find Callie right where she'd left her.

Stepping into the bathroom, she kneeled on the floor next to Callie and rubbed her back. "Hey, what's up?"

A big tear rolled down Callie's cheek and Shelby swallowed the large lump that formed in her throat.

"I'm not supposed to show you."

"Show me what?"

When Callie said nothing further Shelby turned her niece to face her and gentled her voice. "There is nothing you can't show me."

Her voice slightly shook and the fear that began to crawl through her body at what was happening to this precious little girl stole her breath. Leaning forward, she turned off the water, ran her hand through it to make sure it wasn't too hot or cold, then turned to Callie and smiled.

"I promise I won't say anything."

Callie's blue eyes met hers, then she slowly began to pull off her long-sleeved shirt.

Bruises. This precious little girl had bruises. On her arms. On her collarbone. On her back.

Shelby swallowed again. She couldn't stop the tears that flowed from her eyes at the sight of those horrible dark marks on Callie's little body.

"Oh, honey, what happened?"

Callie started crying. "Daddy hit me and told me I was just like my mother."

"Oh." Shelby wrapped her arms around Callie once again. Swallowing, she inhaled deeply. "Oh, that's just the most beautiful thing about you sweetheart. You are, so much like you're mamma. And, it's beautiful."

She held her niece for a while then Callie stood back, finished undressing and climbed into the warm water of the bathtub. Her beautiful sad blue eyes looked into Shelby's. "You won't tell Dad I told you, will you?"

Shelby only shook her head. After a few moments, she calmed herself and whispered. "No, I won't tell him."

Anders walked in. "Can I play in the tub with you Callie?"

Callie looked at him, and nodded.

"Aunt Shelby said she won't tell Dad about our owies."

Anders began undressing and Shelby helped him into the tub, noting that he had similar marks on his back and arms. To keep herself from staring and crying, she pulled towels from the cabinet, and busied herself while the kids splashed in the water and giggled. At least they'd gotten out of their sadness and hopefully that would help them sleep tonight. But, oh how her heart hurt for these two little babies.

Tonight, she'd rest, then tomorrow while they were exploring, she'd hopefully devise a plan to move forward. Her money would run out eventually and they couldn't stay here forever. She worked in a daycare, as she didn't have a college education. She could work retail, maybe another daycare, though that might be the first place Kurtis would look for her. Her hope was to find a job as a nanny, where Callie and Anders would be welcome to spend their days with her and her charges, whoever they were, and she'd home school them. But first, she needed to get further away from Kurtis because while he didn't care much for the kids, he also wouldn't like the fact that she had them or that the decision was taken out of his hands.

And, likely now, he'd be worried the kids had told her of their father's abuse and he wouldn't want that to get out and spoil his perfectly fake reputation amongst his business colleagues.

6

Diego parked in the lot of a grocery store just before the Indiana-Illinois state line. Checking his GPS one last time, he saw the pin at this location.

Tapping his phone, he called headquarters, not sure who was on the phones today.

"Copeland."

Emmy was on. He smiled. "Hey Em, I'm in the parking lot of a grocery store here in Elmhurst, Indiana. What am I looking for?"

He heard some papers shuffling, then keys on her keyboard tapping.

"Shelby was identified from security footage of this store about two hours ago. The kids were with her. They were in the store for about thirty minutes and left with five bags of groceries."

"So, she's staying somewhere close by and possibly for an extended period."

"Yes. Elmhurst has security cameras throughout the town on the streetlights. Her vehicle, a 2019 Ford Explorer, black, was spotted leaving town to the east. Last video image was at 1700 hours."

Diego looked east and started driving out of the parking lot and down the main street area. Elmhurst was a small town and easy enough to navigate.

"I'd guess an Airbnb or short-term rental of sorts. Can you pull those up for me and send me phone numbers and addresses of offices if there are any? I'll be checking in with them."

"You got it. Sending over to you now. There are only three in that area."

"Thanks Emmy. Josephs out."

The line went silent and he glanced as his phone screen lit up with texts coming through. Tapping on the first one he listened as his phone rang over his Bluetooth and his speakers grabbed the signal.

"Hello, Creekside Resort and Cottages."

"Hello. I'm looking for a cottage, perhaps a bit out of town for a few days. Checking on your availability."

"Oh, I'm sorry, I just filled my last place for this week."

"Oh, shoot. I'm now stuck with nowhere to go. Was your last place in a quiet spot? I may be coming back to the area soon."

The elderly voice on the other end of the line paused, then responded. "Yes, it's along the river just out of town. Very peaceful."

"That sounds just perfect. Do you happen to know if there are any other rentals in the area that sound as perfect as yours does?"

The lady laughed. "Of course, not as perfect, but my brother and his wife also have rentals just out of town. I can give you their number to see if they have any openings for you. They aren't on the river, but you could hike through the woods and find the river if you're looking to get some exercise."

"Exercise after sitting in the car for a long time sounds just right."

The kindly lady rattled off the phone number and Diego mentally imprinted it in his brain, memorizing it to call right after.

"Just for kicks, so I can drive by and see where your rental is, can you also give me the address?"

He pulled over to the side of the road, and pulled up his small notebook, quickly jotting the phone number of her brother's rental office first.

"It's just out of town to the east, along the Blue River. The address or fire number is 24498 County Line Road."

"Thank you. I'll check it out and give you a call back."

"Good luck to you, sir."

The lady hung up and he decided first to drive past the address the lady gave him as he called her brother to get another address. With a lot of luck, he'd find where Shelby had the kids. With even more luck, they would be safe and she hadn't done anything to them.

As he exited the little town he found County Line Road and turned onto it toward the river. About a mile out of town he found the little cottage the lady on the phone mentioned. The vehicle outside of the cottage was a red pickup truck and the family gathered along the river didn't look like Shelby and the kids at all.

Dialing the brother's number he listened and planned to go through his conversation again until he'd called all three places in town.

A male voice answered, "Hello, The Cottages."

"Hi. I just got your number from your sister. I'm from out of town and looking for a nice quiet place to stay for a couple of days."

"Well, I just rented my trailer, but I do have a little cottage just up the road from the trailer a bit. It's quite small, only a one bedroom."

"May I have the address of the cottage? I'd like to do a drive by if you don't mind."

The male chuckled. "Not at all. It's just past my sister's place, and around the corner to the right. You'll see a driveway to the right, which has a steep incline, that's for the trailer, but the cottage is just past that driveway about a hundred yards. You can't miss it."

Diego smiled to himself. "Thank you. I'll give you a call back in a few minutes."

He continued past the family at the cottage and soon found the steep driveway the gentleman mentioned. He slowed down but continued driving past, hoping to see something. He didn't see a vehicle, but there were lights on in the trailer as he drove around the corner and soon he came upon the cottage. Deciding fate was with him, he pulled up in front of the cottage and parked in the driveway. There were trees between the cottage and the trailer, but he felt confident he could walk through.

Putting his truck in park and stretching his back muscles, Diego jumped from the driver's seat and opened the back door for Teddy to get out to stretch. He scratched his pup behind the ears and got a couple licks in return before Teddy bounded off to the edge of the trees and promptly peed. Diego chuckled and pulled Teddy's water bowl and the gallon jug from the back of the truck. He poured the water then set it on the ground before grabbing a bottle for himself.

He noted how quiet it was here and checked the time. Around seven thirty. The sun would be setting soon.

Walking around to the passenger side of his truck, he opened the door and pulled his flashlight from the glove box and his phone off the charging stand. Ted was sniffing the area, his tail wagging happily, as he enjoyed being freed from the truck after a few hours of driving. They'd driven across the state of Indiana today and made good time. Ted was the perfect companion, never whining or complaining or griping about the music Diego liked to listen to, which was older rockabilly music. His favorites: Credence Clearwater and Lynyrd Skynyrd.

He lightly whistled for Ted, who bounded over to him, ready to get to work. Ted drank eagerly from his bowl and Diego waited for him to get his fill, then began walking to the edge of the woods toward the trailer to see if he could spot the vehicle in the driveway.

7

A fter tucking the children in bed, Shelby told them their favorites stories, which were made-up stories of themselves. She'd create them as superheroes saving the world and they would giggle and laugh and it made her heart feel full. She sat on the edge of the bottom bunk alongside Callie until she knew they were both asleep. Exhausted, she walked out to the living room and picked up Anders' socks and jacket that had found a home on the floor, and began cleaning up the counter in the kitchen and started the dishwasher. Thank goodness this place had a dishwasher.

Afterwards, she checked that the door was locked, the blinds all closed, and then sat on the sofa contemplating her next move. Her big plan was to make it to South Carolina, where she had a friend from high school she hoped would help her. She hadn't called her yet, because the fewer people who knew what happened the better. Shelby played with a lock of hair that rested on her breast and realized they'd be looking for a woman with long dark hair. It would be the absolute usual thing to do to dye her hair blond; authorities, if Kurtis called them, would be looking for that too. So, she wondered about hiding in plain sight. But, maybe cutting her hair short wouldn't be a bad idea and it could give them a bit of an edge if they needed to get away. She'd buy the kids caps or plastic glasses or something that didn't look too out of the ordinary but also somewhat of a disguise. She remembered making Halloween costumes with her children at the daycare and how much fun they'd had and wondered if an arts and crafts project would be something the kids would like. They could make fun costumes from thrift store purchases; she'd seen one in town.

Happy with the prospect of that idea, she decided to go into town first thing in the morning before town got busy and visit that thrift store and the dollar store next to it. Surely they could come up with some fun costume ideas without spending a ton of money. And bonus if the kids had fun in the meantime.

The next thing she'd need to do was get a different vehicle. Her plan had been to sell this one on her own and use the money to buy another car. Taking her burner phone outside, she snapped a few pictures of her vehicle inside and out.

Hearing movement in the trees, she stopped and looked toward the back of the trailer, unsure what kind of animals were in the woods in this part of the state; her heart raced and her throat dried up. Quickly running to the steps of the trailer, she let herself in and locked the doors. She tried to see whatever it was in the woods from the back window, but dusk had settled and there was no hope of seeing anything in the darkness.

After a drink of water and some deep even breathing, she managed to get her fear under control. Sitting once again on the sofa, she looked at the pictures she'd taken of her vehicle and began crafting an ad with them. It would be a bonus if she could get a good price and quickly so she wouldn't be so afraid to go out. As it was, she wondered about the danger of leaving the car at the grocery store and walking to the thrift store to keep her car out of sight and them separated from it in the meantime. It would depend on how tomorrow seemed to work out for them. She'd have to check the weather to be sure.

Satisfied with her ad, she uploaded it to the internet then shut her phone down for the night. Shelby stood and stretched her back, then walked to the kitchen to turn the lights off. Still wondering what she'd heard in the woods, she peered out of the window once more for anything that seemed unusual. It was difficult to see out there and she'd heard nothing since, so she chalked it up to feeling paranoid and not being familiar with the area.

Just in case, she double-checked the locks on all the windows and the two doors on the mobile home.

She didn't feel secure enough to climb in the tub, so she washed her face and did a quick wash up of her intimate parts before putting on a pair of sweatpants and a t-shirt. The kids were still peacefully sleeping so she quietly locked the bedroom door behind her and for good measure moved the suitcases in front of the door. One thing she hadn't anticipated when she planned some of this out was feeling as if she always had to look over her shoulder.

Kurtis was a monster. He'd shown little care that her sister disappeared and when the police also showed no interest in her sister's disappearance, going so far as to call her a conspiracy theorist, she'd started digging into things on her own. Kurtis had told the police she'd been depressed and when she tried correcting that narrative, she was told she was being hysterical and wouldn't do Stacy any good like that. It was a total set up. When she started hearing the kids say he yelled all the time and punished them for the smallest infraction, she worried about them too.

Then she noticed their behaviors change. They began acting like little robots, making sure nothing was ever out of place, standing with their heads down until they were told they could play; it was heart breaking. Then the phone call where she'd heard Kurtis saying he needed to get rid of Stacy's brats. That call, just yesterday bolted her into action to get the kids and run. She left the house yesterday telling the kids she'd see them today, then she cleaned out her bank accounts and went home and packed, only bringing what she absolutely needed.

She didn't have the money, the power or the connections to beat Kurtis in court for custody, prove he was abusive and mostly to prove he'd harmed Stacy. This was the only thing she could think to do.

Sliding into bed alongside Callie, she rolled to her side so she faced the door and wished she had a gun.

8

H e was certain that was her. Though it was hard to tell with the lighting, but he watched as she went back to the trailer and looked out the window. He'd managed a picture, and looking at it now, it was grainy and hard to tell with certainty. As soon as they settled in for the night, he'd run over and get the make and model of her vehicle and the license plate number and run her tags through the computer.

Kneeling in the soft ground at the edge of the woods, he sniffed the air and could smell the rain rolling in. He'd check the weather on his phone when he was out of sight of the trailer in case she was looking out the windows.

Ted obediently sat next to him, ready for a command. Checking his watch, he saw it was now close to 8:30. A bit early for her to sleep, but if it was her, she'd likely had a stressful day. He'd give it another few minutes then creep over and tag the car and make it back to his vehicle. Then he'd park up on the edge of the road where he could watch that driveway in case she intended to get up in the middle of the night and leave. He'd catch a few winks here and there, he was getting used to it now.

Glancing around the area he could hear the river running through the woods where the other cottages were and he'd check there again just in case but he didn't think that family over there had anything to do with the Kennedys.

Patting Ted on the top of the head he said, ""Shh." Ted slowly followed him from the edge of the woods where they were hiding and they both quietly walked along the edge of the woods in case they had to duck in for cover. Once her vehicle was in sight, he made his way without sound to the vehicle, took a few pictures of it as well as a picture of her plates, then retraced their steps to the edge of the woods and out of sight of the trailer. Allowing Ted his lead, he clicked his tongue. "Go back Ted."

Ted took off running and enjoying himself once again and Diego smiled. He was a damned good dog.

The trek back to his truck was easy and he once again whispered a prayer at his good fortune. He loved this job. He loved how it all worked together and he gave Emmy props for her great business sense. She had help from her dad and her uncle, but she was smart.

Reaching the truck, he lifted the tonneau cover and opened the tailgate and pulled a tote toward him. Opening the tote, he pulled out a tracking device. Closing the tote and pushing it back into the back, he closed the tailgate then pulled the tonneau cover down and latched it. He patted Ted on the head, who sat looking up at him for instruction.

He knelt down to Ted, and lovingly ran his fingers over Ted's face and scratched him behind the ears. "You wanna play a bit bud?"

He unlatched Ted's vest and pulled it off of him. "Okay, let loose a bit, we might be in for a long night."

Ted ran toward the woods, stopping at the edge, his nose down, he sniffed the ground, his tail wildly wagging.

Diego opened the back door and tossed Ted's vest in the back, then he opened the driver's door and sat in the seat, facing the woods so Ted could see him. Using the light inside his truck to see, he began setting up the tracking device and syncing it to his phone. Once he had that in place, he called headquarters.

"Hey Diego, it's Charlesia, what's up?"

"Hi Charly, when did you get back?"

"This morning. Sheldon made me one of his omelets and I fell into a food coma for a few hours. I'm suspicious he drugged me."

Diego laughed. Charlesia had a dry sense of humor for sure, but she was amazing at her job.

"I wouldn't mind if he drugged me once in a while. Good sleeping then."

Charly laughed. "Yeah, for sure. What's going on with you?"

"So, I'm on the trail of Shelby Davidson and the kids she kidnapped. Her niece and nephew, Callie and Anders Kennedy. I think I've found them but I haven't been able to confirm. I'm sending over the vehicle pictures and license plates in just a few. Once confirmed, I'll run over and place a tracker on her vehicle. I've only seen her, not the kids."

He could hear tapping in the background. "Okay, send them over, I'll look at them as soon as they come through."

"Thanks Charly. Are you available if I need assistance or should I call Van?"

"We're both available Diego, just call and one or both of us will be ready, willing and able to help you. Are you expecting trouble?"

"I don't think so. I doubt she's armed, but if she gets skittish and runs before I can make contact, I may need backup."

Sounds of Charly working on the computer came through loud and clear. "Okay, I'm set, load the photos and I'll call you back."

"On their way. I'm out."

He ended the call, then pulled up his email and loaded the pictures. Sending them over. He looked for Ted, who was hard to locate in the dark. His black coat blended with the dark and made him disappear. He whistled and Ted came bounding from the woods.

Good damned dog.

He hopped from the truck and poured more water in Ted's bowl, then pulled a bottle of water and a meal bar from the cooler. Opening one of Ted's food packs he poured his food into another bowl kept in the truck for this purpose and set it on the ground next to Ted's water. He eagerly attacked his food, his tail wagging the whole time. If only people could be so happy and appreciative of a bowl of dried food and water. Life would be easier.

Diego finished typing his report into the computer when his phone rang.

"Josephs."

"It's Charly. So, I have confirmed that is Shelby Davidson's vehicle. Nice work."

"Thanks Charly. Ted and I will run over and put the tracking device on her vehicle so if she sneaks out we'll be able to locate her."

"Sounds good. Let us know if you need help. Charly out."

He hung up the phone and clicked his tongue. Ted, who lay in the backseat resting, instantly jumped up, he wagged his tail furiously and whined, eager to get back to work.

Diego grabbed the tracking device he'd set up earlier and opened his car door. After he jumped from his truck, he opened Ted's door, hooked Ted's vest around his body, then stood back so Ted could jump from the back of the truck.

Diego poured him another bowl of water and watched as he eagerly lapped it up. Sliding his cell phone into his back pocket, Diego grabbed a flashlight from behind his seat, clipped it onto a belt loop, then pocketed the tracker into his front zipper pocket of his vest. As soon as Ted finished his drink, Diego clicked his tongue and Ted bounded after him as they walked into the woods toward the trailer where Shelby Davidson was staying.

The walk only took fifteen minutes, maybe twenty, but it was a fairly easy path between the two properties and he didn't mind the exercise one bit. These were the times when he felt the most alive. He was working a job he'd loved from the beginning. He loved his coworkers. He felt fulfilled in his purpose of helping find children who had been kidnapped and mistreated. His team members felt the same.

As he neared the trailer he stopped and crouched down, scanning the area for anyone outside, or any movement inside. Negative on both.

Running at a low crouch he scooted up to Shelby's vehicle, reached under the driver's side door and stuck the magnetic holder connected to the tracking device to the frame. Standing briefly, he looked in the back seat and saw the two car seats and let out a sigh of relief that the kids were still likely alright if she kept the seats.

Quickly leaving the area and escaping to the edge of the woods, he crouched down low and pulled his phone from his back pocket. Pulling up the tracking app, he activated the tracker then clicked the icon on his phone which communicated with the tracker, which then caused the tracker to emit a red light, then nothing. All set.

Quickly typing out a message on his phone to Charly, he said, "Completed."

Ted dutifully sat at his left watching him and waiting for his next command. Diego smiled at his faithful companion, received a lick on the cheek and chuckled.

"Okay buddy, lets go back and get a bit of sleep."

They walked through the woods, Diego's flashlight shining on the ground to illuminate his trail, satisfied that this matter would be closed soon and the kids would go back to their father, who must be worried sick about them.

He allowed Ted to run just a bit before buttoning up for the night, it wouldn't be the first time they'd slept in the truck and luckily, Ted prefered to be in the truck than stuck at home, so there were no issues with their sleeping arrangements for tonight.

Packing Ted and his dishes back into the truck, Diego climbed in the drivers seat and reclined the back as far as it would go. He messaged Charly once more.

"Car seats in Shelby's vehicle."

He set the alarm on his phone for four hours which would get them to just after one in the morning, then set his phone in the cup holder of his truck, pulled out a meal bar for his dinner, and then settled in for a few hours sleep. Charly or someone would let him know if Shelby's vehicle moved.

***

Diego's alarm sounded and he opened his eyes. Still pitch black outside. A quick glance around the truck showed him nothing had been disturbed and no one had come to see what he was doing here, which he didn't expect, but then again, it was often the case where things you didn't expect were the ones that took up the most time.

Checking that he didn't miss any messages he then moved his seat back to the upright position and rubbed his hands down his face.

Ted stood and lay his chin on Diego's shoulder to get a few scratches and some kind words.

"Morning boy, how are you doing this early morning?"

He was greeted with a few sloppy kisses before Ted looked out the window.

Starting his truck, Diego then pulled his seatbelt across his body and latched it into place, then backed his truck up and pulled out onto the road. He turned left out of the driveway and toward the trailer, slowing as he neared to see if there were any lights on inside. Somewhat relieved that it was dark, he was fully relieved when Shelby's vehicle was still in the driveway. Since she'd purchased several bags of groceries, he assumed she'd planned on staying a while but he didn't want to fully rely on that assumption, since it was just an assumption. He continued to drive down the road, finding a turn around about a mile up, he then turned around and headed back. A few feet from the turn off to the driveway, he parked on the shoulder of the road and settled in to watch for the duration of the night in case she tried leaving.

Resting his head on the back of the seat his body relaxed. He turned his radio on and found a station he liked, always classic rock for him, then turned the volume low so he could hear a vehicle or any noise.

9

Shelby opened her eyes and looked around. The door was still closed and the suitcases were still in front of the door. Callie still slept; slowly turning her head, she could hear Anders snoring above on the top bunk.

She slowly inhaled and rubbed her eyes. Quietly sitting, she hefted herself from bed and walked to her suitcase by the door. As quiet as she could, she moved the kids' suitcases aside and stepped out with hers. The bathroom was in the next room and she hoped the shower wouldn't wake them but she needed to get an early start this morning. She turned the water on to warm, then opened her suitcase and pulled out a clean pair of jeans and a gray t-shirt. It seemed that dressing down would be key, as she usually wore khakis or other type slacks when with the children. Kurtis insisted they look like they were not poor, not that she thought jeans made them look poor, but he had certain peculiarities that she didn't understand. She'd make it a game for the kids today to dress in the weirdest clothes which hopefully would hide them in plain sight.

Stepping under the warm water, she washed her hair, then her body, making quick work of her shower in case the kids woke.

After rinsing her hair, she shut the water off, quickly toweled dry then wrapped the towel around her body. Searching in the drawers of the bathroom vanity she felt lucky when she found an old scissors.

Combing through her hair, she parted it down the middle all the way to her nape and pulled the two sections forward over her shoulder. She'd watched a video on this once and hoped she could pull it off. Combing the left section smooth, she then pinched the strands between her forefinger and middle finger and cut them chin length.

Taking a deep breath as she watched the long strands fall into the sink, she did the same to the other side before she lost her nerve. A couple of snips to make sure both sides were even at her chin, she then combed her hair back and steeled her nerves for the next big task. Bangs.

Parting off a section of hair at the front, she combed it forward and again pinched the hair between her fingers, cutting it at the tip of her nose. That way when they dried, they wouldn't be too short. Fingering her hair around her head, she then rubbed her scalp and let her hair fall around her face. As it dried, she'd play with it a bit and maybe take her curling iron to it to hopefully shape it up.

Scraping the hair from the sink, she dropped it into the toilet and flushed, watching it swirl and disappear, praying she did the right thing. Which said a lot; she hadn't done the right thing by stealing the kids, but she didn't know what else to do.

Another cleansing breath and she began to dress for the day. Once dressed she opened the bathroom door and looked to make sure the kids were still sleeping. She then left the door open so they would see her in here and not be afraid.

After dressing she applied some makeup then pulled her curling iron from her suitcase and plugged it in. Allowing it to heat, she pulled her travel blow dryer out and dried her hair, straightening it with a round brush as she did. Looking in the mirror, she was rather pleased with her new style, though she could tell in the back it wasn't perfectly even. Hopefully she'd be able to have someone straighten it out for her when she got to her friend's house. If she got there. They had so many miles to go and things to do before that time.

Closing her suitcase up, she walked it out to the living room and crept to the kitchen to start the coffee brewing. The clock above the stove said it was 6:00 a.m. And the kids would likely be waking up soon. She'd heard them through the night, a bit fitful and restless, but they went back to sleep.

Pulling her burner phone from her back pocket, she turned it on and waited while it started back up. First thing on the agenda was selling her SUV. That money would get them by for quite some time. She'd buy an older van with a portion of the money and she'd use the rest to live on until she could find them a place to stay and she could get a job. Not having anyone to turn to sucked. Her only living relative now that her sister had disappeared was her mother, who suffered badly from dementia and hadn't remembered her in years. She'd never told her mother that Stacy was missing; she wouldn't understand anyway.

"What did you do to your hair Aunt Shelby?"

She whipped around to see Callie staring at her, her own riot of curls in a horrific state of disarray after sleeping so fitfully last night. Plastering on a smile, Shelby kneeled down and held out her arms to Callie.

"I thought it was time for a change. What do you think?"

Callie touched her hair and smiled. "It's soft."

Shelby smiled. "Shall we comb through your hair and make it soft too?"

Callie only nodded. She walked her to the living room and sat her on the sofa. "Stay here and I'll go get your brush. Maybe you'd like a braid today?"

"Daddy doesn't like braids."

Letting out a breath Shelby responded. "Daddy isn't here today so you can have whatever you want."

Callie's smile broke her heart. "I want two braids."

"You got it girl. I'll be right back."

Shelby settled the kids at the kitchen table with breakfast —pancakes, their favorite. The air in the house grew heavier as the morning dragged on, the humidity increasing by the hour. Her new short hair would be a blessing if it continued on this track. She now realized why she'd gotten a bargain on this place. No air conditioner. The breeze outside increased and she opened the windows which surely helped with the air flow.

Sitting at the table to eat with the kids, she smiled as Anders wolfed down his pancakes.

"Can I play video games please?"

"When you've finished your breakfast."

He eagerly shoveled another forkful of pancakes into his cute little mouth and she giggled. That kid.

"Aunt Shelby are we going to go explore in the woods today?" Callie asked.

"I think that would be fun, don't you?"

Callie shrugged her shoulders and had another bite of pancake. Wanting the kids to stay engaged, Shelby continued.

"I thought we could go to town today and stop at that thrift store. We can find fun outfits and make costumes. I thought we'd have fun dressing in clothes your father doesn't allow. Since he's not here to see us."

Anders sat up straighter. "I'm gonna get a baseball cap like James has."

Shelby looked at him and smiled. "What kind of a baseball cap does James have?"

"He has a green one and it has a G on the front cause he likes the Packers."

Shelby nodded. "So he's a football fan?"

Anders shrugged his shoulders and set his fork on his plate. Turning his light blue eyes to her he smiled. "Games now?"

She giggled. "Yes, go ahead."

Callie smiled. "Me too?"

Shelby glanced at her plate and saw she'd eaten well. "Okay."

Both kids bolted from the kitchen and out to the living room. Shelby cleaned up the dishes, filled the dishwasher and wiped the table and the counter down. Looking at her phone for the time she sighed. It was only 7:30 a.m. Likely nothing was open in town. Unsure of what to do next, she decided to bake something. She'd bought a cake mix at the grocery store thinking the kids would appreciate a treat, and since she'd paid for this place for yesterday, today and tomorrow, they'd be here to enjoy it. She rummaged in the cupboards and found cake pans, but one was round and one was a square. Mismatched everything it seemed here. Oh well, she'd figure something out.

Locating mixing bowls, spoons and a spatula, she pulled the butter from the fridge to grease the pan and, using her grandma's trick, she scooped a spoonful of the cake mix from the box to use in place of the flour.

A gust of wind shook the trailer a bit and a knick-knack on the counter blew over from the open window. Wiping her hands on a towel, she closed the window and looked into the living room to see the kids had stopped playing and were staring into the kitchen.

"It was just a gust of wind kids, it's okay."

Callie nodded and walked to her and gave her a hug.

Kneeling down, she hugged Callie until Anders joined them, then they had a nice group hug. Pulling back she looked Callie in the eyes, then Anders.

"It was just a big gust of wind, really. I'm just going to close some of the windows though so things don't blow around, okay?"

"Okay." Callie whispered then turned to sit back on the sofa. Picking up her game controller, she continued to play and Anders soon joined her.

Shelby watched them for a moment, then proceeded to the bedroom and closed the window in there. She checked the second bedroom and closed both of them. Back in the living room she saw the kids playing again and hummed to herself as she walked to the kitchen. She finished the cake mix, put both pans in the oven and cleaned up her mess.

Setting a timer on the stove, she thought to check her online listing and see if she had any takers on her vehicle. She turned the phone on and waited while it booted back up. She checked her ad: no comments and no email addresses. Crap.

Another gust of wind rocked the trailer and both kids jumped. Maybe they should go to town as soon as the cake was finished baking to get out of the trailer until the winds died down. They could get their fun outfits and once they got back to the trailer, they'd have stuff to keep them busy, maybe get in some exploring too until it was supper time. Sounded like a great day and it would certainly tire the kids out.

She explained their day to them and they both clapped.

"Okay, then, go in the bathroom and brush your teeth and put your shoes and socks on. We only have to wait until the cake is pulled from the oven."

Both kids set their game controllers on the top of the entertainment center then took off running to the bathroom. There was certainly some pushing and racing, but that's what brothers and sisters did. She laughed at their antics and wondered for the millionth time where Stacy was.

The kids finally got their teeth brushed and their shoes and socks on after Shelby hustled them along. The oven timer went off and she pulled the cakes from the oven.

"Okay, now we can get rolling."

She unlocked and opened the door and they bounded out of the house and down the three steps to the ground. Once again racing, their dark hair blowing in the wind.

Looking up at the sky, Shelby shuddered; the dark clouds seemed to be rolling right to their location at breakneck speed. This didn't seem good at all.

10

D iego watched as the Ford Explorer emerged from the steep driveway and turned toward him on the road. Looking down at his lap so his face didn't show, he waited for them to pass, then checked his phone to see if his tracker had engaged. After checking his mirror to see the vehicle round the corner, he started his truck, made a U turn and began following at a distance.

He stifled a yawn and felt Ted's chin rest on his shoulder. He patted Ted's nose. "It's okay boy. All good."

That seemed to satisfy Ted as he then stuck his head out of the driver's side back window and looked up the road.

Entering the little town of Elmhurst, Diego's eyes slid to his phone in the dash holder; Shelby's vehicle had stopped. Watching for the vehicle as he slowed through town, he saw her helping the kids out of the car at the grocery store they'd stopped at yesterday. He drove past and parked at the edge of the lot, partly because he didn't want her to notice him and partly because Ted would need to pee and there was grass at the edge of the lot.

He parked the vehicle but did nothing as he watched Shelby, hands clasped with a kid on either side of her, cross the street and enter a dollar store.

Diego opened his door and hopped from his truck, then opened Ted's door and let him out. Ted quickly ran to the grass, sniffed for the absolute perfect spot and peed. Diego positioned himself to the side facing the dollar store so he could see when Shelby and the kids left the store, but also keeping an eye on Ted. As Ted sniffed the area, Diego poured him water and set his bowl on the ground, then busied himself should Shelby and the kids come out of the store. He didn't want to look like he was watching for them; that could be cause for their alarm.

Twenty minutes later they exited the store with a couple of bags and went next door to the thrift store. Diego's brows furrowed as he wondered what they were up to. The bags didn't look at all like clothing bags and if they were running, why would they buy a bunch of crap?

Ted began rolling in the grass on his back, enjoying his time out of the truck almost as much as he enjoyed his time in the truck. A dog's life was fantastic. Changing off between watching the store and watching Ted, Diego sat in the grass as Ted sniffed, rolled around and sniffed some more. About forty minutes later Shelby and the kids emerged from the thrift store carrying bags. Anders now wore a baseball cap and a large smile on his face.

They crossed the street and walked to her Explorer where she opened the back hatch and they loaded the bags inside. After closing the hatch, Shelby helped the kids into the back and he loaded Ted into the back of his truck.

Diego collected Ted's dish and the water jug and busied himself putting things away so she'd hopefully leave the lot without noticing them. From the corner of his eye he saw her pull out of her parking space and drive toward the trailer they'd stayed in last night. Still not sure she was staying there again, he climbed into the driver's seat, activated his tracking device and after it engaged, he followed her trail.

He sighed as he turned the corner and saw her pulling into the driveway. Since the device was working properly and it appeared she was staying, he decided to secure the cabin for himself and Ted for the night, maybe two. He dialed the number of the man he spoke to yesterday and was relieved the cabin was still available.

Once he'd parked his truck, he walked to the front door and entered the number he'd been given on the keypad; he waited for the beep, heard the lock slide open and twisted the knob to enter his home away from home.

Finding it neat and tidy, he brought Ted and his go bag in from the truck then planned how to make contact with Shelby and the kids without scaring them. He had the perfect partner to do this with—he had Ted. Kids and dogs, they just went together.

Diego set up Ted's food and water, dropped his go bag on the foot of the bed, tossed food from the cooler into the fridge and set out to take a hike in the woods and scope out the area.

The air outside was humid and the aromas of the vegetation mingled in the air adding a fragrant mist. He turned toward the trailer Shelby and the kids were in and hoped he could make contact.

Ted's working vest was still on, which meant he stayed by Diego's side as they trekked through the woods. It was a short distance between the two properties, which was a bonus. The humidity hung in the air and the temperature was rising quickly.

As they neared the edge of the woods he heard voices and halted. Ted sat at his feet looking up at him waiting for his command.

"Aunt Shelby what do you think this is?"

"Let's look it up, I'm not sure."

The sound of turning pages filtered to his ears and he crept forward to get a visual. Peering through a small copse of trees before him he saw them, Shelby and the kids, standing over a flower as Shelby paged through a book.

"It says here this is a Blue Star Willow. See?"

She knelt down by the flower and lay the book in front of it. "What do you think?"

Callie nodded in agreement, "It looks the same."

"Yeah." Anders nodded.

Diego stifled a chuckle as he watched them. Shelby sure didn't look like she was about to harm the kids; it looked like they were exploring.

Anders stepped a few feet away and in his child like wonder exclaimed, "Oh my gosh, look at this!"

Shelby walked over to him and knelt down. "That's an acorn."

"What's that?"

Diego slowly reached down to Ted and unbuckled his vest. Scratching Ted behind the ears he whispered, "Good boy." He stood then and said, "Go play."

As he hoped, Ted bounded for the kids. His thunderous thrashing through the trees had Shelby and the kids turning toward him quickly at the sounds and Diego had to step in quickly so they didn't think Ted would harm them. Stepping from the trees he whistled for Ted which caused Ted to stop quickly.

Diego glanced at Shelby and the kids and smiled. "Hi, sorry my buddy here scared you."

Shelby smiled tentatively, "He doesn't bite, does he?"

Diego held up his vest, "No, he's my therapy dog and I just took his vest off so he could play a bit. He gets excited when his vest comes off."

Anders spoke first, "Can I pet him?"

"Sure, if it's okay with your mom."

Shelby's eyes rounded. "I'm not their mom, I'm their aunt. We're on an adventure."

"I apologize, I didn't mean any harm."

"Oh, no harm done."

Anders walked the few steps to Ted and slowly reached his hand forward. When Ted sat still Anders patted him on the head and giggled.

"He's letting me pet him."

Callie then walked toward Ted and patted his head as Shelby watched the kids carefully.

Diego looked directly at Shelby, "What are you exploring today?"

11

Shelby took a deep breath and let it out slowly. What the hell was a strange man doing in the woods by her rental?

"I thought the kids would enjoy learning about some unusual things today. What are you doing out in the woods?"

The man looked into her eyes. His were interesting. Not the color, but the intensity they held. The color was nice too, though.

"I'm staying in that cottage..." He pointed behind him. "And Ted needed to stretch his legs, we've been in the truck for a while."

"Why does he wear a vest?" Anders asked.

"He's a therapy dog. I have panic attacks and he helps me through them. When he's wearing his vest, he's working."

Anders laughed. "Dogs don't work."

"Sure they do. Ted does."

Shelby watched the interaction and thought he seemed nice enough. But, they didn't need to get too close.

Callie walked forward and stared up at the man. "What's your name?"

He smiled and it was a nice smile. "Diego, what's yours?"

"Callie."

"It's nice to meet you Callie."

Anders continued to pet Ted but said, "I'm Anders."

"Nice to meet you Anders. You have a way with dogs. Ted usually likes to run around when he doesn't have his vest on."

"I like to run around too."

Anders then took off running and Ted followed him.

Shelby called after him, "Not too far Anders."

"Okay," he yelled back, continuing to run with Ted.

Shelby looked up at him again and saw the faint smile on his face as he continued to look in the direction Ted had run with Anders. "He won't get far from you, will he?"

His eyes landed on hers and her tummy did a little somersault.

"No, he stays close. He listens well, too." Diego whistled and she heard the thrashing that she'd heard before but this time it was accompanied by a giggle.

Anders and Ted came back into view and she had to admit, Anders hadn't looked this happy in a long time. He'd begged for a dog since he was two years old, but Kurtis would never allow it.

Callie was more restrained around Ted, but she also had two more years of her father telling her how awful dogs were. It was natural for her to keep her distance.

She looked at the handsome stranger once more. "How long are you staying in the cabin?"

When he looked into her eyes she felt it physically, like a bolt of lightning.

"Just a couple of days. I wanted Ted to get out and run a bit, then we have to go and find a place to get food. I wasn't planning on staying over-night but my company decided at the last minute that I was needed here. I'm just waiting for a call to tell me what my next assignment is."

"Assignment? What do you do?" She watched his face to see if he was a liar.

"I have to report on the area. Telephone systems, cable systems, and other services. Sometimes I have to locate certain objects and pinpoint them on the map."

He'd answered quickly and she didn't detect his evasion.

Anders jumped in quickly. "Why don't you eat with us. Aunt Shelby made a cake."

Her cheeks burned almost instantly. Kids just didn't understand things and Anders was the most loving caring boy she ever knew.

Diego chuckled and she opened her mouth to try and find the words to beg off but Anders struck again. "Ted can eat scraps. I'll share my food with him so he doesn't get hungry. Please Aunt Shelby can they come to the trailer for supper?"

Diego looked at her then smiled, "It's fine if you're uncomfortable; you don't know me. But, I'm on the road a lot and would love the company. And, Ted seems to love Anders. He's likely sick of me."

Her stomach turned and twisted but she was interested in a weird sort of way. He seemed harmless and if someone came around to do them harm, it couldn't hurt to have an ally if she needed one. Please God don't let her need one.

"I did make a cake and we do have enough food. Though, I need to tell you ahead of time it's a no-frills supper. We were going to have hamburgers and baked beans."

"Hamburgers and baked beans sounds wonderful. Can I bring something?"

She shook her head as butterflies took flight in her belly. She felt rather foolish since she was a kidnapper and he was a stranger and she was inviting him to dinner. But there was something about him that spoke of protection, trust, and safety that she hadn't felt in...what? Years.

"No, I've got it. Why don't you come over around five. We're just getting ready to go back now and rest up after our adventures today."

"I could use a rest myself." He whistled and Ted bounded over to him. Anders frowned and Diego chuckled. "I'll bring him back tonight Anders and you can play with him then. Okay?"

"Okay."

Diego looked her in the eye and smiled. "I'll see you around five. I didn't catch your name though."

Her cheeks burned and she felt the heat crawl up her neck. "Shelby."

He held his hand out to shake hers and she tentatively lay her hand in his. The shock that ran through her body was immediate and intense. When he gently squeezed her hand it felt like a hug. A warm, safe hug.

He waved goodbye to Anders and Callie and whistled as he turned away from them and Ted took off following him. She stood transfixed for some time before she shook her head free of its thoughts; she was acting weird. How could a woman, now a criminal, have thoughts so far out in left field when she should be focusing on the kids and staying under the radar? But, part of her thought about the security of having someone to lean on, which had been something she'd dreamed about through all of this. Maybe this was God's way of answering her prayers.

12

At five o'clock, Diego and Ted walked through the woods to the trailer Shelby and the kids occupied. He and Ted had taken a nap, after he ensured his tracking device was working and he'd turned up the volume on his phone so he'd hear it go off if they moved. The first thing he'd done when he woke was check to see the vehicle hadn't moved and he let out a sigh. Now to get inside and see if he could figure out what was going on with Shelby. If he were forced to finalize his report now, he'd say she had no ill intentions toward the kids. Over time he'd developed the bullshit meter as they called it at the compound. You could just tell when someone was out for bad-intent and he didn't get that vibe from Shelby at all.

He walked up the three steps to the trailer door and knocked. He heard Anders cheer and yell, "Ted's here," then footsteps running toward the door.

"I'll get the door Anders, just hang on."

Shelby opened the door only a crack at first and peered out at him. As their eyes met he smiled and she smiled in return, then she pulled the door open.

"Hi."

"Hi, I hope we're not early."

"No, just in time actually."

"Perfect."

He stepped in past her and Ted immediately sat at his feet waiting for a command. He smiled as Anders stood and watched him, his little brows furrowed in the middle.

"Why doesn't he want to play?"

"He's working. See, he has his vest on."

Diego leaned down and took the vest off of Ted, then scratched him behind the ears. "Good boy."

As soon as Diego stood Ted ran toward Anders and Anders laughed. After that, Anders and Ted were joined together. Anders ran down the hallway and Ted followed him. Anders jumped on the sofa and Ted followed, though he didn't jump on the sofa because he wasn't allowed.

Shelby giggled. "Well, it looks like those two are occupied. Can I get you something to drink?"

"If you have a bottle of water, that would be perfect."

Shelby nodded and walked to the kitchen. Not sure if he should follow, he stayed in the living room and watched the kids play with Ted. Actually the kids sat on the sofa and petted Ted and when he'd lick their hands and faces, the shrieks of laughter made Diego smile. They were cute kids and they looked completely happy and healthy.

"Here you go." Shelby handed him a bottle of water and laughed as Anders giggled at Ted. "You are a hit. At least Ted is."

He smiled at her and nodded. "Ted is always a hit, everywhere he goes."

She was a beautiful woman. Her eyes were easily the prettiest green he'd ever seen. The pictures Emmy had of her did not do her justice. Her petite frame was encased in jeans and a loose gray t-shirt but rather than mask her body, they enhanced her slender frame and fitness. When she smiled, she was stunning.

He opened his bottle of water and took a drink, replaced the cap and looked at Shelby. "Supper smells fantastic."

Her cheeks turned the prettiest shade of pink which magnified the dark rich tones of her hair.

"Thank you. We don't have a grill here so I had to fry the burgers but I think they'll be delicious anyway."

Almost as if by magic, Anders said, "I'm hungry."

Callie looked at her aunt and said, "Me too."

Shelby smiled at the kids and nodded. "Supper is ready. Go wash your hands and then you can come in the kitchen."

The kids bolted to the kitchen, Ted in tow and he turned but waited for Shelby to proceed.

The aromas in the kitchen made his mouth water. The table was set for the four of them, and on the counter was a delicious looking chocolate cake on a plate. No frills or decorative frosting, but the icing was crafted in swirls with care and it looked inviting as hell.

"Diego, please take a seat right next to the window."

The table had been turned so no one had to sit with their back to the window, which he knew she had done purposely since it took up more space this way. But, he appreciated being able to see out the window and was grateful for it nonetheless.

13

Shelby cleaned up the dinner dishes and listened as the kids played their game in the living room. They complained slightly less today about not being able to connect to the internet and she was grateful for that.

It had been nice having adult company tonight. Diego was good company. They chatted about nothing in particular and he didn't ask too many questions which she appreciated. He asked them how long they were on their adventure for and that was the only time she felt funny about not having an answer and by that time she didn't want to lie to him. He'd been so kind and Anders took to him almost instantly. That little boy was the sweetest little guy on the planet and Kurtis treated him like shit.

Diego told Anders and Callie stories about Ted and how he got him and how Ted was trained and some stories about Ted as a puppy which both kids thought was funny. Diego even showed them pictures of Ted as a pup and they both thought he was soo cute.

Around six-thirty Diego stood and whistled and Ted walked obediently to his master and sat as Diego affixed his vest.

"Thank you for dinner. It sure was nice having some company."

"It was very nice; I'm glad we ran into each other. I'll say Ted was a huge hit too."

He laughed and Shelby thought how handsome he was. His normal look was intense and wary. His happy face, now that was handsome for sure. It made her want to make him laugh all the time.

As soon as he'd left and closed the door she felt oddly sad that he was gone. She wiped the table off and turned it so it would rest against the wall under the window, after the last of the dishes were added to the dishwasher, then she scoured the sink, wiped the stove off one last time, wiped down the counter and tossed the dirty kitchen rag into the basket in the pantry for that purpose.

A gust of wind rocked the trailer and she froze as she listened to the wind howl through the trees outside. Taking a look out the window the trees danced in the wind. Large oaks and maples with enough weight to have been standing immobile for most of their lives now bent and swayed and it made her nervous. She wished she would have gotten Diego's phone number, but she wouldn't have used it anyway. That would seem desperate.

Shelby stepped into the living room and saw both kids had stopped playing their game and were looking out the window at the trees.

"Aunt Shelby is there going to be a tornado?"'

Shaking her head Shelby sat on the sofa and immediately had two children hugging her closely from either side.

"I don't like storms." Callie muttered into Shelby's left arm, her face buried as much as she could bury it.

"I know you don't, sweetheart. Let me take a look at the weather app and see what I can see."

Pulling her phone from her back pocket, which was a struggle with the kids afraid to move back, she resumed her position as each child tucked themselves in closer.

She opened her temporary phone only to find some of the fun apps she wanted weren't on this phone, so she had to extract herself from the kids for a moment to grab the remote for the television.

Coming back to the sofa, she turned the television on and found a local weather station only to be sorry she did. There was a major storm blowing in and it promised to bring heavy rains, monsoon type winds and damage to the area. She'd never liked staying in a trailer in the first place, but now, she didn't want to be in a trailer at all.

Shelby processed everything she could about the area and wondered if the grocery store would be the best place to be during a storm like this. It was a huge building and likely built in this area for this type of weather. Deciding it would be wise to get rolling before the storm worsened, she squeezed the kids under her arms and said, "I have an idea. Let's go to town and stay at the grocery store during this storm. It's big and safe and it'll be dry. What do you say to that?"

Callie looked up at her, "We'd have to go out in the wind though."

"Yes, but in the car it won't be bad and once we get there, we'll be able to relax more."

As if Mother Nature were warning her, a wind gust blew through so hard it rocked the trailer and Anders began crying.

Shelby stood. "Grab your coats, let's go quickly before the storm gets worse."

14

Diego pulled up the weather app on his phone and knew this wasn't good. Ted had been whining for a couple of hours, his senses assaulted by the change in the air pressure and he was afraid of storms, so Diego knew he'd need to get Ted somewhere secure or he'd have some real trouble on his hands if he had a PTSD episode and Ted was out of commission.

Glancing around, he knew the best place to be was lower, and the trailer Shelby and the kids were in was certainly down the hill and the roof was only a foot above the road, so they were protected. He could likely pull down there and park alongside her vehicle, offering them some protection. At least until the worst of it was over. The wind blew stronger and actually rattled the windows which had Ted whining again.

"It's okay buddy. I've got this."

Diego grabbed his go bag and Ted's food stores and vest and got him to his truck. He started the ignition and pulled out of his driveway, turning left to go to Shelby's trailer. Just as he approached the trailer, Shelby and the kids came out the door and ran to the SUV. She froze when she saw his vehicle and he stopped short of pulling up alongside her SUV.

Putting his vehicle in park, he exited and held his hands in the air.

He pointed with his thumb to Ted, "Ted, is afraid of storms. There's a bad storm coming through and I came down here to tuck in next to your vehicle because it's lower down here."

Shelby looked suspicious, who wouldn't? "Isn't your cabin safe?"

"It's higher than this is and I thought this would be safer."

Just as the words were out of his mouth a wild gust of wind blew through and Ted howled.

Diego walked to the truck and opened Ted's door. "It's okay buddy."

He looked at Shelby. "I wouldn't go out if I were you. It's not safe up there in these gusters."

"What's a guster?"

"These darned wind storms when they blow through. Sometimes they turn into tornadoes. You don't want to be on the road for those."

He glanced at the kids, both standing close to Shelby, the little one, Anders, holding on to her leg.

"Not with the kids for sure."

Shelby reached back and touched both the kids with her hands and they came around to her sides, but she continued to hug them both against her.

"What do you plan on doing?"

He glanced at Ted, "I was going to pull up close to your vehicle, then get in the back with Ted and wait it out."

"In your truck?"

He shrugged, "Where else would I go?" Pointing up to the road he continued, "It's safer tucked into the lower sections of the hills here than it is up there."

Shelby glanced to the road and he watched her process everything. He could see the indecision in her eyes and her protective stance. Then she looked at him and he saw the fear in her face. "They were afraid because the wind gusts rocked the trailer."

He nodded, "I'm sure it's anchored. Want me to look?"

She opened her mouth to say something then closed it, her brows furrowed and another big gust of wind blew through, so strong Anders was pushed against her vehicle.

"Aunt Shelby, I'm scared."

"I know honey." Shelby looked at him, "How do you check to see if it's anchored?"

He pointed to the skirting around the bottom of the trailer, "I can open that up and see if its anchored down. Usually they pour large cement pads." He walked to the side of the trailer and kicked at the ground a bit. Finding concrete under the dirt. "Like this. Before the cement is dried, they stick long metal anchors into the cement, letting them stick up, with eye rings at the end. Then the frame of the trailer is fastened to the rings when they bring it in. The skirting is just for looks and to keep animals out of it."

He pulled back the skirting and pulled his phone up, turning the flashlight on, shining it inside. He nodded, "Yep, it's anchored."

Soon the wind howled and the gusts were no longer gusts, but it was a constant wind blowing through strong enough that Diego had to steady himself against the trailer. Ted howled again and Diego leaned forward to push through the wind to get to his truck. As he walked past Shelby he yelled, "You and the kids should go inside."

She turned without another word and took the kids inside. He jumped into his truck, pulled up alongside her SUV and hoped this wouldn't be too bad.

He then got out and climbed in the backseat with Ted. His shaking pup jumped on his lap, which meant there was a lot of dog on his lap. Ted was part Labrador, part Newfoundland. He was a big boy. All eighty-five pounds of him.

He tried calming Ted down, whispering to him and petting him to calm him. A knock on his window had him jumping and he turned to see Shelby outside, her short hair blowing around.

"You should come in. It doesn't seem right that you and Ted are out here."

"Are you sure?"

"If something would happen, I..." She trailed off and he saw her swallow. She didn't seem like a monster to him.

"Thank you."

He grabbed Ted's leash and vest and his bowls and a dog food pack and they followed Shelby inside.

As soon as the door closed, the trailer shook and the kids huddled together on the sofa, Anders crying. "I'm scared."

Diego felt bad for the kids and slowly approached with Ted in tow. He sat in a chair to the right angle of the sofa and had Ted sit down, though he crawled to sit between Diego's feet.

"Ted's scared too. He doesn't like the wind."

Anders and Callie looked at Ted, who shook and tried hiding his head behind Diego's legs.

Callie inched forward on the sofa and then leaned down. "Can I pet him?"

"Sure you can pet him. He's a good boy. It might make him feel better too."

Anders then scooted forward and dropped to the floor next to Ted. He reached out tentatively and touched Ted's fur, then a big smile formed on his little face.

"I like that he lets me pet him."

Diego grinned. "He loves to be petted. He's also a great companion."

Just as he said that Ted licked Ander's face and the sweet little boy laughed.

15

Shelby stood by the door and watched, second guessing if this was the right thing to do. Though she'd been second guessing herself for the past few years actually. She'd been impulsive on more times than she could count so this was par for the course for her.

Another blast of wind gusted through and the trailer rocked once more. Ted whined and the kids huddled together, fear on their faces. She walked over and sat on the sofa and both kids scrambled to sit next to her as she wrapped her arms around them and held them close. Diego remained on the floor, calming Ted with soothing words.

"It's okay boy, we're all good."

He continued to pet Ted with slow steady strokes. The care he took with Ted was nice to witness. He couldn't be a bad person and care so much for his animal. Right?

"Why is he afraid of the storm?" Anders asked.

Diego looked up at Anders, then at Callie and finally he looked into her eyes. He smiled and she thought it was a nice smile.

"When he was a puppy, before I got him, someone careless left him and his siblings outside in a storm. They were scared, wet and traumatized. Since then, he's been trained to help me when I'm scared, he's such a good boy, but he can't get that bad trauma out of his head. But, I will always take care of him and be good to him. That's our deal with each other."

Anders scooted forward and looked down at Ted. "How does he help you?"

She watched Diego swallow and take a deep breath. "I have PTSD, which is very similar to what Ted has. Sometimes I have bad dreams, or bad memories come rushing back at me and make me shake and get scared. Ted can sense when that's about to happen and he comes to my side, lays his head on my lap, or if I'm in bed, he'll lay across my chest and lick my face to bring me out of my bad memories."

Anders nodded and sat on the floor. He looked Ted in the eye and said, "Sometimes I get scared too."

Ted licked him on the cheek and Anders giggled.

Diego looked at Anders. "What do you get scared about?"

Anders shrunk back against the sofa. "I'm not supposed to say anything."

Diego nodded. "Okay, fair enough."

Diego's eyes darted to hers and she felt her cheeks burn. He likely thought she did something to the kids.

The wind howled, and it continued for a long time. It sounded like a train was running right toward them. It was so loud it was hard to hear and Ted began howling again.

Diego stood, "Is there a room here without windows? We need to get to cover."

Shelby stood taking the kids hands. "Yes. The bathroom."

She tugged the kids to the bathroom, glancing back only once as Diego picked up Ted and carried him. The poor dog shook like a leaf and she felt sorry for him.

After Diego and Ted entered the bathroom, Diego kicked the door closed with his foot then gently set Ted on the floor. Diego fell to the floor in front of Ted, with his back to the door. He then looked at her. In the small bathroom they were quite cramped.

"If you have towels or something for the kids to sit on so it's more comfortable they could sit in the tub."

She nodded and pointed to the cabinet he sat in front of. "In there."

He reached over and opened the cabinet then grabbed a handful of towels and tossed them into the tub. Shelby began opening them slightly then helped the kids into the tub.

"There, that's more comfortable."

Callie finally broke her silence. "Why are we in here?"

Diego smiled at her. "If a tornado comes through, it might break the windows. If we're in a room without windows, we won't get sprayed with glass."

Callie's eyes grew large. Shelby smoothed Callie's hair. "It's okay sweetie. We'll be fine here, we have to have that belief."

"Okay." Callie's voice was small and shook slightly.

Shelby took a deep breath and hoped she was right. When she looked over at Diego, she saw him watching her. His brown eyes were intense and it felt like he was assessing her. She feigned a smile, and it felt fake even to her, so she figured it looked fake to him. His lips thinned and he simply nodded.

The trailer continued to shake, and Ted climbed right up in Diego's lap. Diego wrapped his arms around Ted and held him close, continuing to try and calm him the best he could.

A loud crash sounded outside and both kids began crying. Shelby climbed right in the bathtub with them and held them close to her. She rubbed their heads and backs and kept her eyes closed. Sending up a silent prayer, to God, and to her sister Stacy if that's where she was, to keep them safe, hoping all her prayers would be answered.

Several more loud crash-like sounds happened and the trailer rocked as the windows in one of the rooms popped and broke. The wind howled as it whipped through the trailer, the constant rocking motion of the trailer had her rethinking her quick decision to stay here. If the tornado picked the trailer up and tossed it, they would all be injured or dead.

The wind then died down and an eerie calm ascended on the trailer and the outside as if nothing had happened just a few moments ago. The air pressure changed and the humidity of earlier began to fill their small space once again. Not sure if it was safe to go out, she looked at Diego, who still comforted Ted.

He then looked up at her. "I'll go out and see if it's all clear, but I have to leave Ted here in case there's broken glass out there. I don't want him to step in it."

She nodded and stood. Stepping from the tub she looked at the kids, "Stay right here, I'll sit on the floor with Ted until Diego assesses the situation outside."

Both kids looked up at her with the saddest fear filled faces she'd ever seen and her heart swelled for them. Sitting next to the tub, Diego stood and led Ted to her. Petting Ted to sooth him again, he looked into her eyes. "You may need to continue to talk to him. He'll be worried when he sees me leave the room. Just talk softly to him and keep contact with him please."

Nodding she watched as he turned and stepped quickly out the door, closing it softly behind him.

16

S tepping from the bathroom and into the hallway, Diego's eyes landed on the sparkling shards of glass laying across the living room floor at the end of the hall. The curtains on the windows had blown in and lay inside the frame of the window, dripping water and looking rather ragged on the ends from the glass ripping into the soft-looking material.

Stepping further down the hall he saw the mess that had been made of the living room and the broken glass had been tossed across the width of the room. It lay on the sofa and chairs they'd recently vacated, and he was grateful his good sense kicked in and they had moved.

A quick glance outside showed him the area had suffered some damage, broken limbs from the trees at the edge of the property were strewn about littering the wet ground with leaves, branches and debris from garbage cans around the area. Who knew how far those things had flown?

The kitchen was largely unscathed, though glass had flown throughout the room but the windows were intact. The counter still held two freshly baked cakes now covered in glass but otherwise sitting likely where Shelby had put them before the storm.

Walking to the living room once more he opened the door to the outside and stood staring at the carnage. Large trees had fallen and now blocked the driveway out of here, three garbage cans were intermingled with the branches and other garbage that had blown about.

Diego looked up at the sky and saw the yellow tinted sky was now beginning to brighten as if nothing destructive had just happened here.

He pulled his phone from his back pocket and looked at the weather app to see that the storm had blown through and now had passed on a mile or so south and was breaking up. Derechos Storms were so much like a tornado that it was hard for the normal person to discern, but that's what his app called it. Large and destructive without the extreme power of a tornado. Though looking around it was hard to believe a tornado hadn't blown through.

Pocketing his phone he walked back to the bathroom and opened the door slowly so Ted wouldn't bolt. His eyes landed on Shelby petting Ted and the two kids talking to him and petting him as well. They likely were calmed by keeping Ted from freaking out. Bonus.

Shelby looked up at him and he noticed the green of her eyes like the softest spring grass with a frame of dark full lashes. Her jaw tightened as she waited and he thought she was certainly in a pickle now. Two kidnapped children, though he doubted she meant them harm, they certainly weren't hers, and now with no place to stay. He wondered about her finances but knew it didn't matter because as soon as he could, he'd need to call Emmy and report that he had her and wait for the local PD to come and take Shelby and the kids away.

"There's a fair amount of damage outside. Trees down and windows broken. The biggest issue for us right now is that the downed trees are blocking the driveway out. We'll have to clear them away before we can get out of here."

She swallowed and his heart felt sad for her. He wanted to ask her what she'd been thinking, but had to play his hand close to his chest.

She plastered on a fake smile, "Okay. I suppose we'll need to go out and begin moving what we can."

He looked at the kids, Anders was happy to get out of the tub, likely the bathroom but Callie was more reserved. "What if the storm comes back?"

Shelby tucked Callie's dark hair behind her ear, "If it comes back, we'll come back in here. We'll hear it coming and we'll be fine."

Callie swallowed and he could tell she was nervous. He knelt down to pet Ted and looked Callie and Anders in the eyes. "We made it through this storm and if another one comes, we'll do the same."

Pulling his phone from his back pocket, he tapped the weather app and showed them the clear skies. "That red going south right there?" He pointed, "That's the storm going away from us. And, see all around us, there are no more storms."

Callie looked skeptical, but didn't say anything.

He stood then, "I need to carry Ted out. There's broken glass all over the floor of the trailer, so he can't walk out."

Glancing down at the kids feet, he confirmed that they were wearing shoes, then he glanced at Shelby's feet to see that she was as well. Since they'd all been about to leave, it was a given, but just in case, he did a double check. Better safe than sorry.

Leaning down he softly said to Ted, "Ready boy?"

Ted's tail wagged, though he still wasn't his usual self. It would take a while for him to regain his usual exuberance.

Wrapping his arms around Ted, he scooped him up and bent at the waist and to the left to reach the door handle and twist open the door. He gingerly stepped from the bathroom and through the living room. Twisting the door knob on the front door, he pushed it open and stepped out on the little deck area, then carried Ted down the three steps to the ground. Setting Ted gently on the ground he watched as Ted looked around, assessing his new surroundings. Diego inhaled and the air smelled fresh and clean as if the storm had pushed away all negative smells and left only a fresh new start.

His phone chimed a text and he pulled it from his pocket to read it.

"Kurtis Kennedy isn't on the up and up, we're still digging into him. Wife is missing and he doesn't at all seem concerned. Have you made contact with Shelby Davidson and the kids yet? Emmy"

His heart raced. It would seem there was definitely something interesting going on here. He looked at the door of the trailer and Shelby walked out, holding the kids hands in hers. They carefully walked down the steps to the ground and all of them stood and looked around. The trees had fallen and blocked their vehicles, and Shelby walked to the front of her car and looked at the scratches and gouges in the hood from tree branches as they'd fallen. Her eyes welled with tears and she blinked rapidly to dry them. She turned and looked at the children and inhaled a deep breath, likely to calm herself before speaking. Then she looked at him. "I don't know where to start."

He'd pocketed his phone without answering.

17

D iego looked at his phone again and Shelby began to get nervous.

"What do you do for work?"

He looked up at her quickly, pocketed his phone and said, "My company does computer searches for information on various things. Sometimes we have to go out in the field and locate cars, or places and pinpoint them on a map."

She stared at him for a long time. That seemed like a vague answer but at the moment she wasn't sure what or who to believe and she needed him to help her get out of here. They'd clearly needed another place to sleep tonight.

Swallowing to wet her throat, she inhaled. "Where do we start?"

Watching him assess the area, and walk around the trees to see where the driveway actually was at this point, he walked to his truck and opened the tonneau cover. He pulled a hand saw from the back and looked at her.

"I'll cut the limbs that need to be cut if you and the kids can drag them toward the woods and out of the path of our vehicles so we can get out of here."

"Okay."

He glanced down at Ted and patted him, clearly happy with the tail wag he received in return. He had a nice smile. He didn't use it much, but he had a nice smile. His full lips created the perfect frame for his straight white teeth. He was a man who took care of himself, it was clear. Though his hair was longer, it was clean, well kept and neat. His brown hair and olive skin tone hinted at mixed race, though which ones was a mystery.

She glanced down at the kids and smiled. "Ready to get some work done?"

Anders clapped his hands together, he was always the one who wanted to be a big helper. Callie, not so much.

Shelby led the kids to some downed branches and she picked up the biggest one and began to drag it to the edge of the property, out of the way of their vehicles. She giggled as Anders chattered along as he pulled a little branch and Callie lagged behind with the smallest branch around and carried it with them.

Dropping their branches, they turned to head back to the mess and she stopped briefly when she saw Diego with his shirt off, and in only a tank top or t-shirt. He was built, his muscles well defined and tattoos on both arms depicted trees and roses and she wondered who those were for or what they meant.

The muscles in his arms rippled as he sawed on a branch and it was difficult to look away. His broad chest narrowed to a thin waist and well defined abs and as he lifted his left leg to hold the branch he was cutting, she could see his firm thighs encased in denim - her kryptonite. There was something about a man's firm toned thighs that made her weak.

His saw went through the branch and it fell as he moved slightly to the right to cut the next one. Without looking up he continued cutting the branches and she decided she needed to do her part.

Walking to the branch he'd just cut, she pulled it away from him and dragged it, though not easily, to the other branches. Anders grabbed hold of one of the smaller branches attached to the branch she dragged and smiled up at her. "I'm a good helper."

"You sure are. Thank you so much."

Glancing around she saw Callie grabbing a smaller branch and dragging it behind her and Ted got in the act by grabbing a stick in his mouth and running along side them.

Callie and Anders laughed at Ted and she couldn't help giggling at his playfulness. Apparently he'd gotten over his fear from earlier. Normal activity did that.

Diego had another branch cut from the tree and pulled his phone from his pocket. She watched him read a text and his brows furrowed together.

He tapped his phone a couple of times and put his phone to his ear. "Hi Emmy. So, I'm cutting away at a tree that fell across the driveway I need to get out of due to a Derechos Storm."

She watched him and his eyes turned and landed on Ted. "He's doing better now. He was pretty scared but he got through it."

He listened and she grabbed another branch and hauled it away. She couldn't hear everything he said on the phone but it wasn't her business and she reminded herself she was likely just being paranoid.

He concluded his call. "Okay, I'll call you when I'm able to get out of here."

He tucked his phone into his back pocket and locked eyes with her. "Work."

She nodded and looked around for the kids. Ted was running with the stick in his mouth and Anders was chasing him and Callie was watching them with scorn on her face.

"What's wrong Callie?"

"Anders isn't helping."

Shelby smiled at her. "It's okay, he also isn't complaining that he's bored."

Callie nodded and picked up another small branch and took it to the pile they'd started.

Anders fell into a puddle and began to cry and Shelby ran to him and helped him up. His shirt was covered in mud and some of it splashed on his face.

Kneeling in front of Anders and swiping tears and mud from under his eyes, she smiled at him. "I'll run in and get you a clean shirt. You stay here so you don't get glass in your shoes."

"Okay."

"Don't rub your eyes, you have mud on your hands. I'll bring out a wash cloth."

"Okay." He tried not to cry and she smiled at him.

"I'm so proud of you. This will all be better soon."

She stood and glanced over to see Diego watching her. That assessing gaze on his face again. Her neck stiffened and she hesitated to walk into the trailer. Since he couldn't leave there was no danger of him taking the children, but she got the distinct feeling he wasn't telling the truth.

She stepped into the trailer and gingerly walked across the glass strewn living room to the bedroom. Pulling Anders' suitcase open and picking out a t-shirt for him she then went to the kitchen and found a big kettle. Filling it with water, she grabbed a kitchen towel from the drawer and plopped it into the water. Tossing Anders' t-shirt over her shoulder to carry, she picked up the kettle and carried it to the door, trying not to spill, which caused her to laugh a little bit. Like, why, because she'd make a mess? Look at this place.

18

H e looked up as Shelby walked out of the trailer carrying a kettle of water. Emmy told him that Kurtis Kennedy was not the man he was pretending to be. Not to them anyway and after witnessing Shelby with the children today, he didn't think she meant them any harm. Everything in her demeanor was protective and caring.

She walked to where Anders' stood, Callie talking to him and telling him it'd be alright and Anders trying so hard to be stoic. Kneeling down in front of Anders, Shelby pulled a cloth from the water and wrung it out. Gently wiping the dirt from his face, she spoke to him in a calming manner.

"You're such a good boy Anders. Look how hard you and Callie are working to help us clear the driveway out. That's hard work. Thank you for all of your help."

Anders nodded and Shelby continued to clean his face. Then she dropped the cloth into the kettle and began helping him take his dirty shirt off, holding the worst of the shirt away from his face, she gently lifted the shirt from his body, then over his head.

Diego spotted the bruises instantly on his back, upper arms and shoulders. It made him sick. He glanced at Callie who stood watching him, then she slowly moved herself to stand between he and Anders, blocking his view. He'd guess that these two had been protecting each other for a while now.

Shelby then turned and saw him watching. Her cheeks turned red and her jaw tightened, but she continued to clean up her nephew, gently and lovingly until she could then pull a clean shirt over his head.

The instant Anders was cleaned up and dressed, he took off running and calling for Ted, who'd sat dutifully along side the trio as if he knew he had to watch over them now.

Ted turned and ran after Anders and the young boy giggled. There just wasn't anything cuter than a small child's laugh.

Shelby turned and said something softly to Callie, who nodded in response, then she picked up a branch and dragged it to the others on the side of the property. Shelby stood and watched the kids play and work, a soft smile on her face. His mind instantly confirmed that she was involved in something serious here, but maybe it was for the right reasons.

Shelby tossed the water into the grass, lay the towel over the side of the pan, set the pan on the top step to the trailer, then walked to the next branch she planned on moving without looking at him again. He almost felt sad that she wouldn't acknowledge him.

Guilt also settled over him. He'd lied, mostly by omission, but if he didn't rectify it soon, he'd be setting himself up to a jobless future. His teammates needed to be able to trust him. But, so did Shelby and the kids if he were to figure out what the true sense of all of this was. A woman alone with two small children that weren't hers and with a specified amount of money, of which he doubted she had a lot of, must have had some kind of plan.

Setting his mind to the task at hand, he decided to work a bit harder and release them from this place at least. From there, he'd follow them at a distance and see what he could discern before he reported anything.

Once he'd cleared the tree of the branches he could handle with a hand saw, he put the saw into the toolbox in the back of his truck, then he pulled a tow strap from the back and walked to the top of the tree where it lay in the driveway. Figuring the length to be easily fourteen feet, with the base of it still attached to the trunk on the other side of the driveway, then looking at how much room he would have for his truck to then drive around once he pulled the tree out of the way, he figured he could drag the tree just far enough to clear the driveway.

Glancing briefly at Shelby, he saw her on her phone, texting or doing something. He walked to the top third of the tree and wrapped the tow strap around the trunk of it and locked the hook through the loop to secure the strap.

Walking backwards he kept one eye on Shelby, who now looked up at what he was doing and one eye on the strap to make sure it unrolled without knotting. He then walked around the tree toward his truck. Shelby looked up at him and smiled and he couldn't help but smile at her in return. She was a beautiful woman and one he didn't believe had any ill intent towards these kids. Though at this time she was still considered a kidnapper.

"I'm going to pull the tree out of the way of the driveway, but I don't have enough room to pull it all the way over. While I'm pulling, you and the kids need to stay over toward the other side of the trailer please, in case the strap breaks or comes loose. I wouldn't want any of you to get hurt."

"Okay." She glanced at the kids, playing with Ted. "Kids, come on over, we need to stand over here while Diego pulls the tree out of the way."

The kids ran towards her and she walked to the other side of the trailer where he'd suggested. He whistled for Ted, who came running happily toward him, with a stick in his mouth. Diego laughed at his buddy and opened the back door of his truck. Ted happily jumped inside. They only had about an hour or so of daylight left, so he sent up a prayer that this tree would move easily and he'd be able to get them out of here. Though, he still had to figure out how to respond to Emmy and not lie while watching Shelby and the kids until they knew for sure about Kurtis Kennedy.

Closing the back door, he climbed in the driver's side, clicked his seat belt into place and started his truck. Slowly backing from his parking spot, he then turned the truck sharply to the right to move around the top of the tree, careful not to sink into the mud the rain had created.

The ground was uneven and the truck rocked back and forth, but he kept both hands on the steering wheel and maneuvered around the tree and got into position on the other side of it.

Climbing out of the truck, he forced himself not to look at Shelby, instead focusing on securing the end of the tow strap to the back of his truck. Confident he had everything in place, he looked up at Shelby and nodded. She nodded in return, each of her arms wrapped around one of the kids, touching their shoulders with her hands, huddled together watching him.

He yelled over. "Give me a thumbs up when I've moved the tree enough to drive our vehicles out of the driveway."

"Okay." She yelled back.

Climbing back into his truck he let out a long breath and started it up. Slowly moving forward until he could feel the pull from the tree, he then locked in the four-wheel-drive. Slowly he added pressure to the gas pedal. Nothing happened at first, but then the truck grabbed at the ground and he slowly felt the tree move so he gave the truck more gas and dragged the tree until he heard her yell, "Okay."

Twisting in his seat, he looked back and saw that she was waving at him and he jumped out of the truck and walked to the back, where he looked the area over, and decided he'd made enough room for them to drive away. A little tug in his heart at the thought, but he had the tracking device on her truck so he'd find her easy enough if he didn't follow her. That thought alone made him feel somewhat better and he worked at getting the strap removed from the tree.

Once finished he rolled his strap up, tucked it securely into his tool box and jumped back into his truck. As he rounded the top of the tree, he saw Shelby and the kids loading up their suitcases and grocery bags into the back of the SUV.

19

L ooking up at Diego, Shelby felt bad. He'd
worked his butt off to help them get out of here
and she was packing up the kids the instant he'd
moved the tree.

Looking at Callie and Anders she said, "Kids, get into the
car and I'll go and thank Diego for helping us out."

Anders looked up at her. "Can't I say good bye too? And I
want to say goodbye to Ted, he's my new friend."

Feeling deflated she smiled at him. "Of course, go ahead
and say goodbye."

Anders ran toward Diego, Callie walked toward them but
she was more reticent.

Shelby smiled as she watched Callie. She was so much
like her mom. Someday she'd make sure Callie and
Anders both knew how much their mother loved them.
Right now, it was difficult for her to talk about Stacy
without tears in her eyes. She felt helpless and frustrated

that no one would help her and she didn't have the money to launch an investigation on her own. It wasn't right. The police should want to find a beautiful mother of two who'd just disappeared.

Taking a deep breath Shelby walked toward Diego. Ander's excited chatter to Ted took over the silence between the rest of them and Diego's smile as he listened to Anders was spectacular to witness.

His eyes turned to her when she neared and her heartbeat sped up. "Thank you Diego, for your assistance in getting out of here. I've texted the owner of the trailer and explained what happened and that we've gone to a hotel. If you'd like me to let him know your name so he can pay you for moving the tree, I'm happy to do that."

Diego shook his head. "No need. Thank you for allowing Ted and I a place to ride out the storm. We appreciate it."

Anders' giggles as Ted licked his face turned all of their attention to the pair who'd struck up quite the friendship.

"You're welcome. I couldn't let you face that in your truck."

Diego nodded at her, but the way he stared at her was both unnerving and exciting. Her heart began to race and her breathing grew shallow.

"Okay kids, we've got to get to the hotel before dark."

Anders hugged Ted around the neck, then looked up at Diego. "Ted likes me."

Diego chuckled. "He sure does buddy. Thank you for helping me calm him down during the storm, we both appreciate it."

"Okay." Anders then patted Ted once more and began walking to her SUV, Callie right behind him.

She hesitated for a moment. "Well, thank you Diego. We've got to get going but I do appreciate your assistance."

He nodded, his longish brown hair falling from where he'd tucked it behind his ear. Turning to Ted, he whistled and opened the back door of his truck and Ted jumped right up into the back end. Diego patted Ted's head, received a big lick in return, then he closed the door.

"I'll wait for you to leave to make sure you don't have issues getting out of here."

She smiled, her heart still going crazy. "Thank you."

Turning she walked back to her SUV, feeling terrible about the secrets she was keeping but also knowing they were necessary. He seemed like a nice man.

Leaning into the SUV, she buckled the kids in their seats, then lifted their suitcases into the back of the SUV along with the groceries she'd salvaged. Closing the lift gate, she walked to the driver's side door and climbed in. Buckling herself in, she looked in her mirror and saw both kids staring at her.

"We'll go and find a hotel to stay in for the night, then we'll decide where our next adventure leads us, deal?"

Both of them nodded, but said nothing else and she dreaded the days to come because even though she knew Kurtis wasn't the kindest father and clearly their bruises came from him, she was also lying to the kids and she worried they wouldn't trust her after a while. Going back wasn't an option though so, they had no choice but to move forward.

Putting her vehicle in gear, she glanced up to see Diego watching her from inside his truck and the guilt flooded her body and tears sprang to her eyes.

Inching past the downed tree and up the steep driveway to the road, she glanced to the left to make sure nothing was coming, then she gunned her vehicle and made it up onto the road. Looking down at the roof of the trailer, she saw a tree laying at the back of the trailer, which was what likely broke the windows out of it. Heading towards the next town up ahead, she sent up a silent prayer there'd be a hotel in that town and they'd have an opening. They only needed one room, so hopefully it'd be fairly easy to find one. Fingers crossed.

The silence in the vehicle made her feel worse than if the kids were playing their games and having fun and she felt like something had just happened to change everything.

"You guys can play your game until we get to the hotel if you'd like."

Callie looked at Anders and Shelby watched in her mirror as Anders just shrugged.

"That's okay Aunt Shelby. We'll just sit for a while."

She'd recalled all the times the kids had begged for a dog and Kurtis had always yelled and said he'd never have an animal in the house. They were filthy and full of germs. She couldn't help but think he was the filthy creature in that house and kids needed to have a loving environment to grow up in. Having a pet to love and take care of was such a great experience for kids. She and Stacy had always had dogs growing up. Sometimes more than one at a time, but those days were over.

The road sign said, Crest Hills, 15 miles. They could make it with forty minutes of daylight to spare. Once they settled in for the night, she'd have a few moments to herself to think and plan out what tomorrow would bring. Hopefully.

20

Diego didn't want to scare Shelby, so he allowed her to have a several minute lead. In the meantime, he opened his tracker app and followed her from a great distance. He saw the tracker leading her to Crest Hills and he hoped she'd stop there for the night. He needed to contact Emmy and tell her something. Though right now he didn't know what he'd tell her.

His phone alerted him to a text and he briefly saw the name on the text - Charly. He inhaled and let his breath out slowly. He didn't want to lie to her either. Any of them for that matter. He also didn't want to get fired, but he just couldn't turn Shelby over just yet, what would happen to them if this was all a big mistake? The bruises on Anders and the way Callie shielded him spoke of two small children taught to protect each other, yet they weren't afraid of Shelby.

He neared the city of Crest Hills and pulled into a gas station to fill up. That would give Shelby time to find a place for the night and get there without risking her seeing him. He pulled up to a pump and hopped out of his truck. Pulling his credit card out he knew RAPTOR would know where he was from this purchase and he knew he had to say something and soon. His gut twisted slightly as his next course of action swirled around in his brain. He felt the uneasy sensations building up in him just before he had another attack.

Ted stuck his head out of the back window and whined and Diego reached up and patted his pal on the head. Ted licked his hand and nipped lightly at his fingers. His job was to warn Diego when he was about to have an attack and he likely felt like he wasn't doing his job if he couldn't get to Diego. They were both in the same boat right now.

The pump clicked and Diego turned his attention to the nozzle, pulling it from his truck and setting it back in the pump. His vision dimmed slightly and he knew he had to get into his truck. Pushing the button on the pump he focused on his breathing while both hands rested on the pump to steady himself.

Finally his receipt printed and he grabbed it, turning to his truck and climbing in the driver's seat. Ted's head immediately lay on his shoulder, adding the comforting weight to him that always calmed him down. Hearing a horn honk, he looked in his mirror to see an impatient patron waiting for the pump. Reaching forward he started his truck and slowly moved it to the edge of the parking lot, putting it in park and turning the ignition off. Locking all the doors he sat with Ted's head on his shoulder, his head against the head rest, his eyes closed, focusing on his breathing.

A few minutes later, Ted licked his cheek and he opened his eyes, letting them adjust to the light, which was beginning to dim with the setting sun. A quick glance at the clock on his dash showed him nearly ten minutes had passed.

Reaching up he patted Ted's head. "I love you boy. Thank you for helping me out."

Ted's tail smacked the back of the seat as it wagged. Mission accomplished.

He started his truck, looked at the tracker on his phone in the holder on the dash and saw it had stopped. Tapping the screen, he saw Shelby's location and tapped the location to get the directions to where they were stopped.

The title on the directions said, "Double D's Motel".

"We're stopping for the night hopefully Teddy boy."

Ted's tail wagged again and Diego put his truck in gear and eased out of the parking lot of the gas station.

He found Double D's easy enough. It was just off the main road, and Shelby wasn't much of a covert operator, at least that helped him right now, but if she was running, it would help anyone else find her too. She'd left her car right in front of door number 5.

Parking his truck down the parking lot and far enough away that he wouldn't be noticed, but close enough that he could watch Shelby's vehicle, he tucked in for the night. The motel wasn't filled, as a matter of fact only Shelby's vehicle and one other at the far end of the Motel was in the lot. Getting out of his vehicle, he walked to the passenger side of his truck, which was parked next to a small patch of grass. He let Ted out to go to the bathroom, then he pulled his food and water out of the cooler and let him eat and drink. All the while he watched Shelby's vehicle and her door.

A car pulled into the lot and slowed as it passed Shelby's SUV. Diego watched with interest as the vehicle then pulled to the edge of the parking lot directly across from Shelby's SUV, alongside the grass where he was. A man wearing all black; a black hoodie, black pants and wearing black gloves caught his attention. Diego, clicked his tongue and Ted bounded into the truck. Closing the door, Diego quietly said, "Stay."

He eased his way toward the Motel, though a few doors down from Shelby's room. Acting nonchalant he walked toward her room, trying to act like a motel guest as he watched the man from the corner of his eye walk toward Shelby's room from across the parking lot.

The man stopped alongside Shelby's vehicle, looked inside, then pulled a handgun from his waistband and inched forward. He stopped dead when he saw Diego walking toward him, and twisted slightly so his gun didn't show. Diego pretended not to see the gun and stopped just before the door prior to Shelby's, sitting on the dirty plastic chair just outside the door and pretended to tie his shoe.

The man watched him but made no other move. Finishing his shoe tying task, Diego stood and walked past Shelby's door, then ducked behind the candy machine to watch.

The man inched forward toward her door, and twisted the knob, finding it locked. He knocked then and waited but no one answered. The man knocked again and finally Diego could hear Shelby ask, "Who is it?"

"I need help ma'am."

"I can't help you. Go to the office." Her voice shook.

"Let me in."

"Go away."

At that point, the man lifted his foot and kicked at the door, just above the knob. Shelby and the kids screams could be heard and the man kicked again.

Then the man shot at the door knob, three shots, then kicked at the knob again.

Diego ran toward the man, who then turned to see him, and raised his gun at Diego. Without a second thought, Diego shot him in the chest, three times, until he fell to the ground.

He knocked on Shelby's door, watching the man still laying on the ground and praying they could get out of here without a lot of commotion.

"Shelby, it's Diego, this is an emergency."

"Diego? Did you shoot at the door?"

"No, I shot the man who was shooting at the door and we have to go."

He could hear her wrestling with the knob and figured it was likely damaged from the assailant shooting at it.

"Step back and I'll kick it in."

Lifting his leg, he kicked at the knob and the door swung open. Shelby and the kids stood staring at him, their eyes huge, the kids huddled behind Shelby but peaking around her legs, tears streaming down their cheeks.

"Grab what you can and let's go. No time for explanations now."

Indecision played on her face, but Diego looked down at the man on the ground and Shelby instantly started grabbing their clothing and items on the bed and tossed them into the open suitcase. Zipping it closed she grabbed it off the bed, then the other by the door and ushered the kids to Diego, who held his hands out to them in a plea.

21

Her heart raced and her eyes filled with tears. What on earth is going on?

Diego pointed to his truck. "Get in my truck, we need to leave your car here."

"But,..."

"You're being tracked."

She didn't say anything else she just grabbed the kids hands and ran to Diego's truck.

Diego lifted Anders then Callie into the front seat of his truck. She jumped in behind them as Diego picked up Ted's dishes and tossed them and their suitcases into the back of the truck.

He jumped in then and they sped from the parking lot and out onto the road. They were all silent for a long time. She was afraid to say anything, especially in front of the kids who still thought they were just having an adventure, though this was far from the adventure she'd expected or intended. But, thinking on it now, what could she have offered them?

Finally, the children had started crying softly, as if their brains had caught up with events, she still had her arm around their shoulders, afraid to let them go but they sat in stony silence.

Diego briefly glanced over at her then back to the road. "Who's after you?"

"Why do you carry a gun?" She shot back at him.

The kids both looked up at Diego waiting for an answer.

"I'm a special agent."

"For who?"

"Raptor. We're hired to find missing persons."

Anders looked at Diego, 'We're not missing."

Diego shot a glance at her and she shrunk back into the seat. Her stomach twisted as everything came crashing down around her. She blinked furiously to dry the tears that wet her eyes. She was going to jail and the kids would go back to Kurtis who would harm them like he did Stacy.

She swallowed and took a deep breath to keep her voice from shaking. "Please don't take us back. Things aren't what they seem."

"What are they?" he shot back.

She looked down at the kids who both looked at her for her answer and she froze.

Looking at Diego she responded. "Can we talk about this later?"

He didn't say anything but she saw him nod his head. He pulled off the highway and onto a country road, but continued driving. Thoughts raced through her mind so fast and furious that she had a headache. At some point she knew she'd have to say something to the kids but she'd hoped she could get some information from them first. When was the last time they saw Stacy? What did she act like? Did they hear anything suspicious?

Callie started crying again then, softly, but Shelby felt her shoulders shake.

"Hey there, it's alright honey. I'll do anything I can to make sure you're alright."

Callie lay her head against Shelby's chest and cried while Shelby held her head to her. The tears fell then, silently down her cheeks and she listened to Callie's sobs, though she was trying to be quiet. For such a young girl, she had mature behaviors.

Diego slowed and turned down another road. There were no street lights on this road and the area was dark, the only illumination the headlights shining on the road ahead of them. She was afraid to ask him where they were going but for some reason she didn't think he'd hurt them. If he was going to do that, he had the opportunity at the trailer. But so many questions rushed her, why was he at the motel? But she suspected he'd been sent to find her and the children.

Callie began to settle down and Shelby looked at Anders who was sitting still as can be, though he'd stopped crying. She squeezed his shoulder and he looked over at her.

"Are you alright Anders?"

His eyes glistened, still wet with tears and his chin quivered. "Come here bud."

Anders scrambled past Callie and climbed into Shelby's lap. She hugged him with her right arm as she held Callie with her left.

"I'll never let anything happen to you two if I can help it. I promise you with my whole heart that I will protect you with my life."

Both children huddled into her body and she let her own tears flow.

Soon they entered a small town, only a few street lights were lit, most of the businesses were closed for the evening, but there stood a lone motel, just before the town proper began. Diego pulled into the motel parking lot and looked over at her.

"Stay here please and lock the door when I get out. I'll be right back."

She looked at him and nodded.

He pulled the keys from the ignition and jumped out of the truck. She pushed the lock button as she watched him open the door to the lobby and disappear inside. Waiting only a few moments he walked out of the door and headed to the truck. She unlocked the doors and he climbed inside. Quietly turning the truck around, he found a room at the far end of the motel and parked the truck along the side of the motel, where it wasn't readily visible from the road.

He climbed from the vehicle and she opened her door. First setting Anders on his feet on the floor of the truck in front of her, she slid her legs to the side then jumped down from the truck. Her stomach twisted but her head hurt and she was only slightly hungry. They hadn't eaten since breakfast. The kids had a snack in the SUV on their way to the motel today, but that had been it. She wasn't taking very good care of them. That thought made her heart feel heavier than it already did. She'd promised them she'd make sure they were alright. That meant, good nutrition too.

Reaching in she lifted Anders out of the truck, then Callie. They walked to the back of the truck where Diego was lifting their belongings out. She took their suitcases and Diego tossed a backpack over his shoulder, then hefted a cooler from the back of his truck.

Stopping to close up the tailgate and tonneau cover of his truck, he lifted the cooler once again and walked to the end door of the motel. Unlocking it, he pushed it open and stood back, letting her and the kids enter first. He then propped the door with the cooler and left for a moment as she looked around the room.

It was clean, two full sized beds covered in faded orange bedspreads with floral patterns on them. A sofa sat across from the beds, a television sat on top of a small refrigerator. The bathroom was to the back of the room. The carpets were old but clean the vacuum marks still showing from having been cleaned.

Soon Ted bounded in and Diego stepped in the room behind him, moving the cooler and closing the door.

"This is our home for the night, You and the kids can take the beds, I'll sleep on the sofa."

22

D iego looked around the motel room and figured it would work out for tonight. He needed to contact Emmy and the rest of Alpha Team. He'd ignored their texts so far but they would eventually send someone out to find him if he didn't check in. That would make all of this so much worse.

"Have you all eaten anything today?"

Anders shook his head a bit and lay his hand over his tummy. Shelby looked at him, her beautiful face so crestfallen.

"We had breakfast then a meal bar on the way to the motel. I'm afraid our cooler was in the motel and we were getting ready to eat when..." She glanced at the kids. "The commotion started."

Diego pulled his backpack off the floor and lay it on a bed. "I have meal bars. I can run and get something from the lobby. They had vending machines. I'm afraid a town this small is likely closed up for the night."

Anders walked to the foot of the bed as Diego pulled the meal bars from his bag. Spying the meal bar with a picture of an apple on it Anders pointed to it. "I like apples."

Diego smiled at him. "It's yours bud, go ahead."

Anders took it in his hand and turned to look at Callie. "You like apples Callie."

Callie nodded and Anders handed her his meal bar. He turned and looked at the bars on the bed once again and found another one with an apple on it. A huge grin appeared on his face as he took that one and turned to sit on the opposite bed. Wrestling with the wrapper Shelby knelt down in front of him and opened it for him, then handed it back to him with the wrapper still encasing the bottom of the bar.

Callie got her bar open and sat next to Anders. Both kids kept looking at the door and he realized they were likely afraid after what had just happened at the other motel. Walking to the sofa he pushed it against the door so that the arm of the sofa blocked the door somewhat.

"How about that? Better?"

Both kids nodded and continued eating their bars. He looked at Shelby. "Eat. You need to stay healthy."

She opened her mouth to say something, then must have thought better of it. Taking a meal bar in her hand she opened it up and sat on the bed opposite the kids. He then opened his cooler and pulled out bottles of water for them. After they were all situated, he opened up a meal pack for Ted and fed him, pouring water from the gallon jug he'd had in the cooler for him. Ted made quick work of his food and then curled up alongside the sofa as if he knew that's where they'd be sleeping tonight.

They ate in relative silence and once they'd each eaten, he looked at Shelby and said, "We need to talk about this now."

The kids looked at her, their eyes, such a pretty shade of blue, especially with the dark hair surrounding each of them, and so earnest and pure. His heart hurt for these kids.

Shelby's lip quivered and she looked at the kids, leaned forward and took their hands in hers.

"Callie and Anders, I love you both so much, I need you to know that."

They nodded their heads but didn't say anything. Shelby took a deep breath. "I took you away without your father knowing where we were going. I think he's been hurting you." She looked into their little faces and both children teared up.

Anders looked at Callie. "We're not supposed to tell."

Callie looked down at Anders and wrapped her arm around his shoulders. "We need someone to help us. Momma always said, stick together and tell someone you trust if something bad happens."

Anders nodded and turned to Shelby just as a big tear slid down his cheek. Shelby's eyes welled with tears then but she let the tears fall.

"Your momma was my sister and my best friend. I don't know what happened to her but I think something bad happened. She'd never leave you two. Not if she had any say in the matter. Never."

Callie swiped at her nose and Shelby reached over to the bedside table and pulled a tissue from the box and helped her wipe her nose.

She then turned to look at him. "I took the kids because I overheard Kurtis on the phone telling someone he needed to take care of Stacy's brats." She glanced at them, then back to him. "I think he's behind Stacy's disappearance. He's been hurting the children. I was afraid he'd make them disappear too."

The kids moved to sit on her bed with her, each of them holding on to her with all their might. "I didn't think it through very good. I didn't have a lot of time. He still allowed me to babysit them in the mornings and I knew I had to act fast."

He let out a deep breath. "What makes you think by taking care of you that meant something nefarious?"

"His tone of voice. The finality with which he said it. And the fact that he hasn't seemed worried or bothered that Stacy is gone. He hasn't looked for her and then suddenly the police stopped looking for her. I couldn't get anyone to talk to me about her disappearance. Everyone just clammed up."

"So you took that as a sign he had something to do with it?"

She kissed the tops of the kids heads and held them close to her. "She never would have left these two. Never."

He took a deep breath and let it out slowly. Glancing at the children who were both looking at him as if a silent plea for help he said softly. "Has your father been hurting you? You need to tell me so I can protect you."

Anders looked at Callie as if seeking permission. Callie whispered. "It's okay Anders."

Anders stood and walked the two steps to Diego. He pulled his shirt up and though he struggled a bit, he managed to get it off and over his head.

"He hit me hard. Said I was a brat and shouldn't be alive."

Diego's eyes watered as he looked into Anders eyes. "You should be alive. You're a wonderful boy. And you're so brave too."

Anders nodded. "I want to be alive."

A sob broke from Shelby's throat, and Diego had a hard time holding his emotions together.

Diego held his arms open and Anders stepped into them. He hugged Anders' little body, so small and fragile and certainly not a little body that should have to suffer abuse. There were some sick sons of bitches out there in this world.

Clearing his throat, he looked at Anders and Callie. "Okay, so I need to call my boss and tell her what you've told me so she can help me keep you safe. Why don't you guys get ready for bed while I do that."

Shelby stood and swiped at her eyes. She cleared her throat. "How about a warm bath and then we'll see if we can find something on television to watch before we go to sleep."

Both children walked obediently towards the bathroom and Shelby turned and looked at him. "Thank you."

He shook his head. "I haven't done anything yet."

"I beg to differ. I believe Kurtis planned on having us killed, which would have allowed him to get away with Stacy's disappearance too. I'm the only one asking questions."

Shelby stepped into the bathroom and he heard the water in the tub turn on. He listened for a moment as she helped the kids get undressed, found towels, and pulled their pajamas from their suitcases.

He then pulled his phone from his pocket and dialed headquarters.

"Where have you been Diego?"

"Charly, listen, things aren't what they seem?"

"No shit. We've been trying to get in touch with you on this. Kurtis Kennedy doesn't seem to care that his wife is missing. I had Cyber team look into Stacy Kennedy's records and it looks like she used her credit cards at gas stations around the country, then the last one in Mexico. The issue is, if you were running and hiding, why would you use your credit card?"

"Exactly. What did Cyber find?"

"All the transactions have been placed there falsely. If you track them back to their IP addresses they all go to computers from Kennedy's company, SmartTech. Luckily, we have a crack cyber team who figured this out."

"So, where do we stand now? Kurtis is dirty? What about Stacy Kennedy? What about Shelby and the kids? I have them here with me, but someone just tried to kill them at the motel they were staying at. I took care of him though and got them out of there. But, we'll need Emmy or someone to smooth this over with local PD."

"Shit. Okay. Give me the deets and we'll see what we can find from here. In the meantime, are you set for the night?"

"Yeah. But, I suspect we'll need to keep moving tomorrow. Bright and early we'll be rolling to somewhere."

"Stay put till we get back to you."

23

She tried half listening to Diego's conversation. She still wasn't absolutely sure he was going to help them, but for the time being, they needed to stay out of sight and he seemed as though he was trying to help them.

The kids were subdued and quiet. This had been a lot for them to handle and to admit. She spoke to them softly, smiled to reassure them, but in the end, they all just needed rest. Maybe a good hardy breakfast in the morning. Then she'd need to figure out how to get her vehicle back so she could sell it.

"Aunt Shelby?"

She looked down at Callie. "Yes, honey."

Callie swallowed. "I love you. Are we in trouble?"

"No honey, you aren't in trouble."

Callie nodded. "Are you in trouble?"

Shelby stared into Callie's light blue eyes. Her sister's eyes. "I might be honey. I took you and Anders from your home. That's against the law. But, I'm very hopeful that Diego will be able to help us."

"Okay." Callie let out a deep breath. "I'd like to go lay down now."

"Okay."

She pulled a towel from its resting place on the closed toilet lid and opened it up. Callie stood and Shelby immediately wrapped her in the towel and lifted her from the tub. Callie dried herself off while Shelby did the same for Anders. Getting both kids dressed, teeth brushed and them settled needed to be calm and quiet so they could relax and sleep. So all of her actions were calm and methodical. When they emerged from the bathroom, Diego lay on the sofa, his head at the end of the sofa next to the door, facing them as they walked from the bathroom.

He smiled at the kids. "Who smells fresh and clean?"

Anders giggled and Diego's smile grew. He was a handsome man, if not a bit quiet. Kurtis was a loud boisterous man with a booming voice. He'd always weirded her out with how loud he spoke.

Shelby pulled the covers back on the bed and both kids scrambled to climb into bed. She covered them up to their chins then softly said, "Would you like a story tonight?"

Both kids nodded and she smiled. "Okay, let's start with A little boy named Anders and his big sister, Callie."

They loved it when she told stories and included them as the heroes in them. "Anders and Callie encountered a big bad wolf. He hurt them and they didn't like it. The wolf told them not to tell anyone what happened and they didn't. Not at first, but then one day both Anders and Callie got brave and they told Diego what happened and Diego helped them get away from the big bad wolf. Now, Callie and Anders have a great life with their very own dog and cat, and they live in a house with a big yard where they run and play, and have fun. They have friends who come over every day to play in the yard with them too. Their friends say that Anders and Callie are the best friends they've ever had."

Both children smiled but didn't say anything, their eyes were locked on Shelby's as they listened intently to her helping them forecast their futures. She truly hoped that's how it would end up for them.

"Should I try to find some cartoons on television?"

Anders nodded but yawned, and Callie just shrugged.

Shelby turned the television on, flipped through the channels, of which there were surprisingly many in this little town. She found an acceptable cartoon for them to watch and then turned the light off on their side of the room.

Her eyes turned to see Diego watching her every move and heat crawled up her body at his scrutiny.

He sat up and motioned for her to join him on the sofa, so she sat at the end of it, tucking her short hair behind her ear and now being more self conscious than ever at what she must look like right now. It hadn't been a concern of hers all day.

He leaned forward, his elbows on his knees, staring at his hands folded together between his knees loosely.

"I need to know what possessed you to take the kids and run. Is there something else I need to know besides what you've already told me?"

She swallowed as she watched him from the side. His longer hair dipped forward as his head bent but she could still see most of his face. He was a handsome man, reserved, but she could tell he was smart. He liked thinking before saying anything. It was admirable actually. God she hoped they could trust him to help them out.

She spoke softly, glancing every so often to the kids to see if they were listening. One thing she'd learned, they were almost always listening.

"I think Kurtis had Stacy killed."

"That's quite a statement right there. Why would he do that? Why wouldn't he divorce her instead?"

"They didn't have a prenup. His company is now worth millions."

He turned his head without moving the rest of his body and his eyes were intense. "Did Stacy ever tell you she wanted out of the marriage?"

"Many times."

"Why didn't she just leave?"

"She didn't trust that he wouldn't try to cut her out of everything. The kids too. And, she believed he had a girlfriend too. So, she wanted to make it miserable for him to be with her."

"Why did she think he had a girlfriend?"

"She saw a receipt for lingerie she didn't get. She saw an email for a hotel reservation at a posh hotel in Florida and she wasn't invited and actually Kurtis lied and said he had business in California. Things started to add up."

"Do you know who the girlfriend is?"

She whispered. "No."

She sat still, watching his face as he processed everything. His eyes darted from the floor, to Ted to her than to the kids. Always aware, taking everything in.

Finally he sat back and looked at her. "What was your plan?"

"To get as far away as we could, then sell my vehicle for money and buy something less expensive. Then I'd hoped to make it to South Carolina. I have a friend there from high school. We aren't super close but I hoped that would be good and no one would think to contact her. Then, I'd change our names, get a job and live free from Kurtis and the kids wouldn't have to live in fear."

Diego leaned in and his voice grew quiet. "Didn't he want the kids?"

She shook her head slowly. "Stacy..." A sob threatened and she didn't want the kids to see so she stopped and took a deep breath. Swallowing she waited until she calmed. "Stacy did. He said one. They'd have one. But, Stacy got pregnant with An..."

Tears welled in her eyes and Diego disappeared into her watery vision. She stood up and grabbed a tissue from the box on the bedside table. Luckily, the kids had fallen asleep and didn't stir. She let the inane cartoon continue because it muffled their voices. Dabbing at her eyes she swiped at her nose, then sat on the sofa again.

"When she got pregnant with Anders, Kurtis was livid. Stacy hoped he'd come around but he never did. Things just got worse and worse. The kids came first for Stacy and Kurtis didn't like that. At all. He bitched about everything. Her body changed. Her stamina changed. They left toys out, she was forever running behind them petrified he'd come home and see a toy laying on the floor. It was like living in a prison."

"Fucker." Diego mumbled and she felt better that it seemed as though he truly was there to help them.

"Why were you at the motel?"

"We were hired by Kurtis to find you. He said you'd stolen the children because you couldn't have your own and you'd always been jealous of Stacy for having them."

She shook her head and swallowed. "I wasn't..." Sniffing, she tucked her short locks behind her ear again, "I'm not jealous. I love them. I promised Stacy if anything happened to her I'd take care of them. Always."

"Is it true?"

His voice was tender and he genuinely seemed to care. But, that question always felt like a knife entering her gut slowly.

"I can't have my own. But, I was never jealous of Stacy. She let me be part of the children's lives from the beginning. I was in the delivery room when she had each of them. I've been there to help every step of the way. I love them like they're mine."

Diego sat quietly and her gut twisted. The longer the silence went on the more she worried he didn't believe her. Of course it looked bad.

"Please, don't turn us in." She whispered.

24

His fingers began shaking as Shelby's words lay heavy on his heart. Ted stood and pushed his nose under Diego's hands, then he put his front paws on Diego's knees and leaned into him. Diego hugged his pup, petting him gently and breathing deeply until this episode, small though it was, passed. Ted's head lay on Diego's shoulder, putting as much of his weight on Diego as he could.

Closing his eyes he waited until the shaking stopped. Until his hearing came back to normal. During an episode he sometimes felt underwater, unable to hear clearly.

Once he felt better, he patted Ted's head. "Good boy, buddy. Thank you."

Ted licked his cheek a couple of times then lay at his feet again.

Diego looked over at Shelby, her eyes round with surprise as she witnessed this remarkable thing that Ted did for him.

"Do you have them often?"

"Not like I used to. I used to fight them. Stiffen up, get mad at myself. It made them worse. Therapy has helped tremendously. Ted has helped more."

"Wow. That was something."

He swallowed. "I guess we're both damaged in some way."

He stared into her eyes. They were a beautiful shade of green. Almost the shade of a new grass in the spring. Her dark hair was straight, recently cut short, but very appealing. When she tucked it back, it opened her face more and you could see the full effect of her complexion, the whole picture together was striking. She was beautiful.

"I guess." She looked at the kids sleeping in the bed across from them. "I don't want them to be damaged any more than they already are. They don't deserve it."

He looked to the kids then, their innocent faces so peaceful in sleep. Their dark hair against the white pillow cases such contrast. But they were so tiny they were barely noticeable in the bed as they slept. Little puffs under the blankets.

"I agree. We'll do what we can. My team is working on some things tonight. In the morning, very early, we need to get going. We'll stop somewhere for breakfast, maybe here in town, then I'll wait and see what work wants me to do from here."

"What do you do for work? You said special operative. What does that mean?"

"We work under the radar, so to speak. We go in and do what the police and military can't. Finding children is our specialty, but we've also had to go in and find adults and miscellaneous things. My boss is a badass chick who has lived this life since she was five. Her father and grandfather started a separate group much like us. Only difference is my teammates and I are all wounded veterans."

"Wow." She rubbed the back of her neck with her hand. "It makes me nervous that you've been hired by Kurtis. How do I know you aren't trying to bring us back to him?"

"You don't I guess. But I can tell you, our cyber team found that someone from Kurtis' company faked Stacy's credit card use. We traced it back to the IP address at SmartTech. So they know he's up to something no good."

She covered her mouth with her left hand, her eyes rounded and her breathing increased. "I knew it." She whispered it, but he heard it.

"Get some sleep Shelby, we'll need to get rolling early in the morning."

She stood slowly and walked to the bathroom. After she closed the door he pulled his phone out and texted Charly and Emmy.

"She's protecting the kids. We need to help her."

Emmy responded first. "Right. Come back here in the morning. We've got a room here for them while we figure out what Kurtis Kennedy is up to."

"He was beating the kids."

Charly responded. "Fucker."

"Yeah."

He stood and walked to the clothing rack close to the bathroom where an extra blanket lay folded neatly on the rack. He pulled that down and walked back to the sofa. He'd brush his teeth when she finished.

No sooner had he thought it than the door to the bathroom opened. She walked out, dressed in sweatpants and a t-shirt. She was a sexy woman. Slim in build, her short dark hair allowed her shoulders to be visible and they were slender but strong. She walked with straight posture and a confidence he'd bet she didn't know she had. She still wore a bra, but her breasts were lovely, what he could tell, and she had the nicest ass he'd seen in a while and he worked with some nice looking women.

Her eyes landed on his and she smiled, clearly uneasy about how this was working out. He got up and grabbed his toothbrush from his bag, along with the tooth paste Siobhan had packed up in a go bag, and walked to the bathroom. Using the toilet, then washing up and brushing his teeth, he planned on getting some sleep and dealing with the rest of this tomorrow.

When he walked out, Shelby lay in her bed, facing the children, one of the pillows from her bed now lay on the sofa where his head had been.

"Thank you for the pillow."

She smiled. "You're welcome."

Something just happened to him there. Her soft smile, soft voice and the way she looked at the kids while they slept, that tugged at his heart. Glancing at the kids he smiled. They were cute kids and well behaved too. For such little ones they didn't whine or cry much and they'd been through things most kids never witnessed in their lives.

Glancing once again at Shelby, his eyes locked with hers for a few moments and his heart began racing.

"Good night Shelby."

"Good night Diego."

She reached up and turned off the light and he walked to the sofa, careful not to step on Ted.

25

She heard Diego roll over on the sofa and she couldn't stop thinking about him over there. She didn't feel nervous or scared, in fact, she felt perfectly safe. In her adult life, she'd been a pretty good judge of character. She was the one who practically begged Stacy not to marry her jackass of a husband, Kurtis. Stacy told her she was wrong and Shelby doubted her ability to judge character the first few years of Kurtis and Stacy's marriage. But things changed when Stacy wanted children. After a couple years of begging, Stacy had gotten Kurtis to agree to one child. She was over the moon excited and they set out to get her pregnant.

Kurtis' change continued throughout Stacy's pregnancy. He was incredibly superficial and how she looked and dressed was more important to him than her health. He'd scream and yell at her if she had a day where she didn't look impeccable. It made Shelby sick. She knew then she'd been right about him all along.

But, he continued to grow his company, SmartTech, and spent more and more time away from home and growing further away from Stacy. When Callie was born, Kurtis was less than thrilled. Dirty diapers and a tired wife only deepened his disinterest in his growing family.

Desperate for Kurtis to re-engage with the family, she poured herself into making him happy. And, ultimately she got pregnant again. Something Kurtis was so angry about. Now they'd have two small people in the house to take care of. How could she be so stupid?

Ted got up and walked to the children's bed as Shelby watched him look at them, sniff a few times, then go back to lay alongside the sofa. She thought it was sweet that he wanted to check on them.

Diego moved on the sofa again and guilt washed over her. The sofa was likely uncomfortable. But, it would be weird if he were to sleep in the same bed as she did. It wouldn't look right. She could sleep on the sofa. Wondering if she should offer, her eyes closed.

Hearing Diego move again, Shelby opened her eyes to see him walking into the bathroom. Looking at the digital alarm clock on the table next to the bed she saw that it was 4:00 a.m. Very early in the morning, but he'd said they needed to get rolling early this morning.

He exited the bathroom and she sat up in bed. He walked to the bedside and whispered. "I have to take Ted outside and allow him some exercise. I'll check out the area for food and come back here in a while. Feel free to continue to rest. I'll stay where I can see the door so you and the kids are safe."

"Okay. Thank you."

He pushed the sofa away from the door, then opened it to allow Ted to walk out, he then squeezed through the opening and silently closed the door behind him.

Laying back in the bed she allowed her thoughts to take the direction they wanted to take. Wouldn't life be lovely if she had a man like Diego in it keeping her and the children safe? For that matter, it would be wonderful if Stacy were still alive and she had a husband who wanted to take care of her much like Diego. If money were no object and people were good and nice and genuine. Such pipe dreams were folly for sure. Her father would say she needed to come back down to earth.

Closing her eyes she sent up a silent prayer that if her father was with Stacy right now in heaven, they'd watch over her and the kids so their lives were good. She didn't want to go to prison that was a fact. But even less, she didn't want Kurtis to have the kids back. It was worth risking prison to keep them safe.

She lay there a while longer and her mind continued to shift from thought to thought and the more she tried to make them stop, the more wild they became until her last thought had been one of her walking into a women's prison and the nasty catcalls from the inmates. That scary thought had her heart racing and her body suddenly needing to run or move or something. Quietly getting out of bed, she walked to the bathroom and closed the door as quietly as she could.

Using the toilet, washing her hands and brushing her teeth, she then raked a comb through her hair, somewhat satisfied that she'd done an alright job when cutting it, but feeling like she missed her longer hair too.

Shaking her head because she was wasting energy on something so silly, she exited the bathroom and began packing up the things she could, her toiletries and discarded clothing from last night. She then pulled out another pair of jeans and a clean t-shirt. Ducking back into the bathroom, she changed clothes, folded her soiled clothes up and exited the bathroom once again. Walking out into the room she saw Diego once again sitting on the sofa a steaming cup of coffee in his hand.

He smiled at her and nodded to the bedside table where another cup of coffee sat for her with two sugar packets and a creamer packet lay alongside.

"Thank you." She whispered as she walked to her coffee.

He simply nodded and sipped at his coffee. Ted hopped up on the foot of the children's bed and lay at the edge of it. Poor boy had slept on the floor last night, he deserved a more comfortable spot to sleep on.

Picking up her coffee cup, she added the creamer to it, then replaced the lid. The first sip was hot but oh so good. Simple pleasures.

They drank their coffee in silence until his phone vibrated and he pulled it from his back pocket while looking at the kids.

His voice was quiet, just above a whisper when he answered. "Josephs."

26

H is eyes followed her across the room to her cup of coffee. She was graceful in her movements. Sitting quietly on the bed and pouring the creamer in her coffee, she then set herself back against the headboard and took her first sip. Her eyes closed for a moment and he saw the appreciation on her face. She'd likely been worried about things for some time now. Stacy had disappeared more than a month ago.

"What do you remember about the last time you saw Stacy?"

His voice was lowered and he regretted putting that crease into her forehead when the worry crashed in on her again.

Lowering her coffee cup to hold it in her lap, she let out a breath. "She was planning to take the kids to the zoo the next day. I was there helping her make cinnamon bread. The following morning, we were going to make home-made french toast with the cinnamon bread, then pack lunch and go to the zoo. We thought we'd finish the day with dinner at the restaurant with all the animals in it. Some jungle themed place she'd read about and we thought the kids would have a ball looking at all of them. Then, we'd bring them home tired but happy. We did daily excursions like that on my days off."

"So nothing out of the ordinary for Stacy?"

She shook her head. "No. She complained quietly about Kurtis and his girlfriend, but I think she'd resigned herself to the fact that he was gone, so to speak, and that they'd have to figure out how they moved forward. She told me that would come and she was determined to make him ask for the divorce."

He took a sip of his coffee and waited, not sure if she wanted to tell him more or not. Apparently she did. "When I left the house that day, she smiled at me and hugged me tight. She said, "Tomorrow is going to be the best day ever.""

"What happened the next day?"

A tear slid down her cheek and she let it fall. "I got to the house and the kids were crying. Kurtis had been yelling at them all morning. Nothing they did was good enough. When I asked him where Stacy was he said she left and left him with the brats. Then he stormed out of the house and said, "I have work to do, I assume you can stay with them." I went upstairs to Stacy's closet and many of her clothes were gone. But it didn't make sense. It was like a huge section of her closet had clothing missing but not things a person would take if they were packing up to leave for good and not the things you take if you're leaving for a while. Like a big armful of things had been pulled from the closet without thought. All of her jeans were there. All of her shoes were still there except her favorite tennis shoes. Her underwear drawer had been completely emptied which made no sense but not her sock drawer. Her toothbrush still in it's place in her bathroom vanity."

"Did you tell this to police?"

"Yes. They wouldn't listen to me. Kurtis hadn't filed a missing persons report. Said they had a fight and she took off. I kept calling and they told me she'd been using her credit card. But, I knew she hadn't. A woman who left her children wouldn't be buying coffees and going to movies and buying pieces of art. She never used her card to buy socks or jeans or clothing items she hadn't taken with her. I asked and asked."

"Was a missing persons report ever filed?"

"No. He insisted she left. They said I couldn't file a report."

He finished his coffee and looked over at the children. "I hate to wake them up, but we'll need to get going soon."

"What about my vehicle? Can we go back and get it?"

"Not yet. I'm waiting for my team to let me know what's happening with the guy who tried to kill you. Once I know we're clear, we can go back and remove the trackers from your car and then get it back for you. It's likely in police custody now anyway."

She swiped her hair from her temple, and lay her head back against the headboard.

Her eyes opened and she stared into his eyes. "Trackers? You had a tracker on me too? That's how you knew where we were."

"Yes." There was no need in lying to her.

She took a deep breath and set her coffee cup on the table next to the bed. Scooting to the edge of the bed, she switched to sit on the children's bed. Gently she smoothed Callie's hair back and softly said, "Good morning Callie girl."

Ted moved to lay between the kids, gently sniffing Anders' ear. The cute little giggle that Anders had got Ted stirred up and he began licking his cheeks, his tail wagging swiftly. Anders' arms wrapped around Ted and he said through his giggles, "Morning Ted."

Callie's eyes opened and she rolled over to look at her brother and Ted, her small hand reached out and petted Ted's head, earning her some kisses from Ted too.

Shelby stood and began pulling clean clothing out of their suitcases for the children, laying them on the foot of her bed. Then she pointed into Callie's suitcase.

"Toiletries. Socks. Clothing in sets. Brush. Comb. Extra shoes. This is how a suitcase is packed. If the intention is to purchase items later, they are purchased. You don't buy a porcelain figurine, and coffees at a posh shop. Toothbrush. Socks. Toothpaste. Shampoo."

He locked eyes with her and nodded. She was right in all of that. Even when he and his team went on the road, Shioban made sure they had toiletry bags with a toothbrush, toothpaste and floss in them.

Callie stood from the bed and Shelby handed her clean clothes to wear and Callie dutifully carried them to the bathroom and closed the door. Anders played with Ted a bit more and Diego opened the little fridge in their room and pulled out a small bottle of orange juice he'd gotten from the vending machine.

"Do you like orange juice?"

Anders nodded vigorously and Diego walked it to the bed and twisted the top open for him. Anders took a drink and smiled up at Diego. "Mmm, it's good."

Diego laughed. "Glad you like it bud."

He then looked at Shelby. "I'll start packing up the truck if you want to get the kids ready to leave. I'm told by the maintenance guy here that there's a restaurant about four miles out of town that has the best breakfast anyone could want."

27

The restaurant wasn't very busy, a few truckers sat sleepily at the counter sipping their coffee and waiting for their breakfast. There was a parking lot full of semis at the back, likely many of them still sleeping in their trucks, waiting for the moment they were legally allowed to drive again.

The sweet waitress had greeted them at the door and told them to pick their choice, table or booth. The kids thought a booth seemed like so much fun, so they took the one at the back of the dining room. Diego and Anders on one side, she and Callie on the other.

"I want pancakes." Anders gleefully exclaimed.

Callie nodded. "Me too."

She smiled at them. They'd slept remarkably well last night and today they were fresh and ready to tackle whatever was to come. Hopefully nothing like they'd encountered yesterday. She was still reeling from that. She hadn't slept as good. Likely Diego didn't either because she heard him every time he moved on the old sofa. Poor guy. But, her mind also reeled from all that had transpired. Besides the kidnapping, which she had to admit, she did, there was also the storm, Diego, Ted, the man trying to break in to their motel room, Diego said, to murder them, then Diego murdering said man and them all running. Life had become exhausting.

A waitress stopped at the table and smiled at the kids. "You kids know what you want?"

Callie smiled at her. "We both want pancakes."

Anders spoke up. "And chocolate milk." Then he looked at her and in his sweetest voice asked, "Can we have chocolate milk Aunt Shelby?"

The waitress looked at her and she smiled and replied, "Of course you can have chocolate milk."

The waitress wrote it down on her green order pad. "And for you two?"

Shelby replied, "I'll just have two eggs over easy and a side of bacon. Oh, and coffee please."

Diego had been sitting quietly, but then again, so far that was how he was. He smiled at the waitress when she looked up at him and her lips quivered a bit but never creased into a full fledged smile.

"I'd like the Chef's Special Omelette and coffee."

The waitress wrote that down then asked, "Anything else?"

Diego leaned forward. "I have a dog in the truck, and I carry a gallon of water in a cooler for his water dish when we stop. Would you be able to fill it with cold water?"

"Of course." Her eyes darted to the truck and Ted's big head looking at her from the backseat.

Diego looked at her and nodded. "I'll be right back."

He scooted from the booth and walked to the door and Shelby tried to ignore the heat in her cheeks. This all seemed like something normal and regular to do. It felt familial and sort of intimate. She'd thought of Diego as a man, of course, especially last night. She chalked it up then to hero complex or something because he'd swooped in and saved them. Something she hadn't thanked him for. She'd do that today. When she thought about the fact that they'd all likely be dead if it hadn't been for Diego, she got chills, so she tried putting it from her mind. It hadn't happened but it could have.

There was no doubt in her mind that Kurtis had somehow orchestrated it. If she and the kids were dead at the hands of a burglar or something, it would solve all his issues. At least the most pressing, which was her questioning where Stacy was and why he wasn't concerned and being free from the kids, who he'd never wanted in the first place. Likely the new girlfriend hated having to compete.

She watched as Diego opened his truck and patted Ted's head, then reached in and pulled the gallon jug from the cooler he kept on the floor behind the driver's seat for Ted. When he turned to close the door his eyes landed on hers through the window and she shivered. His gaze was intense and he had a way of looking like he could see into her soul.

She focused on her breathing to calm herself so she could behave normally, whatever that was. But she heard his footsteps approaching the table from behind her and her nipples pebbled and heat crawled up her body. When he sat again at the booth, he smiled at her and she danged near wet herself. What she wouldn't give for a Xanax or something right now, not that she knew how that would help her, but she'd heard Kurtis snapping at Stacy a time or two telling her to take a Xanax and get over herself. To her knowledge, Stacy never did because she was worried about the kids.

The waitress brought their coffees and chocolate milk for the kids and she inhaled the freshly brewed elixir. There was something comforting about inhaling the scent of coffee. It made her think of normal and soothing.

The waitress then lay a placemat in front of each of them and a few crayons so the kids could color their placemats and play the word search and maze games on the back of them. The front of them each had four cartoon pictures they could color. Anders got some space drawings which he loved and Callie had doll pictures. She was fine with them but looked over often to see what Anders was doing.

Smiling as she watched the kids, her eyes then landed on Diego, who sat quietly watching her. He received a text which he quietly read, then responded to without saying anything to her. It was then she wondered if he was married or had a girlfriend. He hadn't told her much about himself except his PTSD and his job.

He glanced at the kids then at her but said nothing. She wondered if he wanted to say something but not in front of the kids. She appreciated him not wanting to scare them.

The waitress brought their food and they ate in relative silence. That was until Anders asked, "Where are we going today?"

Diego answered him. "We're going to my town, Lynyrd Station, where I live. Then we'll decide."

"Are there other kids to play with there?"

"There are some next door and there are a few more that visit next door. We'll go over there and play with them."

Callie set her fork down and took a sip of her chocolate milk. Once she'd swallowed her milk she looked at Diego. "Do you have kids?"

Diego chuckled. "No, I don't have kids."

"Why not, do you like kids?"

"I absolutely like kids, but I never had anyone in my life who wanted to have kids with me."

Anders looked at him with big round eyes. "My daddy didn't want kids but my mommy did."

Shelby choked on her breakfast, her eyes watered as she stared at Anders. Taking a sip of her coffee, she cleared her throat and reached across the table for Anders' hand. "Your mommy absolutely loves you and Callie with her whole heart."

Callie looked up at her. "But she left us."

Shelby shook her head and paused as she gathered her thoughts and her emotions. How did you respond to little children whose lives were so upside down?

"She didn't leave because she wanted to. And, I'll work my whole life to find out what happened to her and where she went."

Diego responded then. "I'll help you."

28

D iego read the text from Emmy and wanted to hurry them along without scaring the kids.

Finishing his coffee, Diego waved the waitress over and Shelby immediately grabbed for her purse. "Please let me get this Diego. It's the very least I can do."

"No. I've got this."

The waitress brought their bill and took empty plates. She came back quickly and Diego handed her the gallon jug that was mostly empty to fill with cold water for Ted. He also handed her some money. As soon as she walked away, he said, "I have to use the restroom and then I'll go out and feed and water Ted and let him have a little walk. You all use the bathroom quickly then we've got to get on the road."

Just as Diego left for the restroom he saw the waitress bringing Ted's water to the table and he nodded his thank you. He'd leave her a nice tip.

After using the toilet and washing his hands he walked out to the main cafeteria and saw the booth empty and instinctively glanced at the truck. They must be in the bathroom.

He grabbed Ted's water jug and walked to the door when the waitress called after him to give him change. He nodded to her, "The rest is for you and thank you." He raised Ted's jug then turned and walked out.

At the truck he opened the back door and let Ted out. He'd parked next to a patch of grass and Ted did his business while Diego pulled his dishes out and filled them. Then, he called Emmy.

"Hey Diego, I assume you got my text."

"Yeah, so what's going on back in Crest Hills?"

He watched Ted and at the same time watched the door of the cafe for Shelby and the kids.

"So, we're watching the activity there and it's being ruled a gang war or drug deal gone bad right now. The victim had GSR on his hands so they know there was some sort of a shoot out or disagreement. But, cops are now looking for Shelby and the kids because her vehicle was there and there was food inside the motel room but she and the kids are gone."

"Okay, so we need to stay out of sight?"

"Yes, and to make things more interesting, Kurtis Kennedy called this morning. He knows about the shooting. He asked weird questions like did our guy find Shelby and the kids? Where are they? He got word that they were near Crest Hills. There's no way he'd know all of that unless he hired the man you shot."

"Right, and I suspect they had a tracker on Shelby's vehicle before I did. I never looked for one when I put mine on because at the time I didn't think I needed to. That could have gotten them killed."

"But it didn't, you were there. Don't go down that road."

He was quiet as he watched Shelby and the kids walk toward him. Ted bounded over to play with the kids and they both laughed and ran with him to the truck. He watched Shelby walk toward him. Her slender body looked fantastic in the ripped jeans she wore. Her short hair gleamed as the sun peeked over the horizon and casted an orange glow on each of them.

Emmy's voice took on a softer tone. "I'll let you know what else we find out. Right now, we're monitoring Kennedy."

Shelby stopped on the grass and smiled as the kids and Ted ran around the small area enjoying themselves.

Emmy's voice broke into his musings. "Diego, how are you doing?"

Inhaling he turned his attention to the kids. "I'm good. Only small episodes and Ted's got me covered."

"Okay. Van and Charly are ready to come and help if you need them. Call immediately if that happens."

"I will. Thanks Em."

He ended the call and looked over at Shelby.

"We've gotta go."

She nodded. "Okay everyone let's get in the truck."

"I wanna sit in the back with Ted." Anders stated.

Shelby looked up at him and Diego nodded. "I think that would be nice for Ted."

She lifted Anders into the back of the truck on the passenger side, and strapped him in. They hadn't taken the car seats and he worried about that, but they hardly had the time.

At least this way Anders was in the back and they weren't so crowded in the front seat.

Once he got them to the compound, they'd get some car seats and figure the rest out.

He lifted Callie into the middle of the back seat and she needed only a little assistance in buckling her seatbelt, then he lifted Ted's dishes and dumped the remaining water from the bowl and set the dishes on the driver's side back seat floor next to Ted's cooler.

Once he'd situated Ted behind him, he climbed in the truck at the same time as Shelby and they both buckled up and he backed them out of their parking spot.

Once they were on the road to Lynyrd Station he looked over at Shelby and quietly said, "Police are looking for you all."

He glanced at Callie who stared straight ahead but didn't make any movements to suggest she'd heard. He knew that meant nothing though, kids were always listening.

Shelby nodded her understanding and he kept driving. They'd be in Lynyrd Station in 3 hours and hopefully they wouldn't have to stop before then. His truck would be able to go that far without fueling up again and other than one of the kids needing to stop to go to the bathroom, they should be able to make it without incident.

Once they'd gone close to halfway, traffic slowed on the highway to a crawl. As they inched along he finally could see what was ahead, there was a check point up ahead. This could mean trouble for sure.

His phone rang and Diego touched the answer icon on his steering wheel, "Yeah."

"Diego, it's Van. We're watching your progress and there's a check point up ahead. Police are looking for Shelby and the kids."

"You have an alternate route for me?"

He chanced a glance at Callie and Anders in the back seat. They both looked nervous and he felt bad for them going through anything more but it was unavoidable.

"Hang tight, there's a turn off up ahead, I'll make sure it's clear."

He worked to make sure he didn't show fear, the kids needed calm. Ted sensed something weird and lay his chin on Diego's shoulder. Diego smiled and patted his head.

"It's all good buddy."

Ted's tail wagged and he sat back and looked out the window.

Van's voice came over the speakers once again. "Okay, up about a half mile is the exit for Grand Ave. Take that, it will swerve you around through a little town on the outskirts of Bloomington, but that will work because you have to head southeast anyway. I'll send you an updated route from there."

"Thanks Van. Turning off in a minute."

Diego put his turn signal on and prepared to turn off the highway. Flashing lights rolled up behind him and he held his breath, then said to all his passengers.

"Stay calm and don't make any sudden moves."

Callie whimpered and Shelby turned and whispered, "It's all okay. We're okay."

29

The police car swerved around them then kept going through the stop sign up ahead, though it did slow to check for traffic, then careened out of sight. She let out her breath and Callie lifted her head. A quick glance at Diego and she saw his shoulders relax a bit and she felt better. His phone chimed a text and he tapped an icon on it. A map came into view and she watched their progress. Van must have sent the new route.

"You have some efficient coworkers."

He smiled before he answered and she thought he had the nicest smile. It changed the seriousness of his facial expressions to that of an extremely handsome man. She liked it.

"I have the best coworkers. They are crazy smart, all of them. Sometimes I have imposter syndrome working with them, like it's a mistake that I work there with them. You know?"

His eyes landed on hers for a moment and she nodded. "I know the feeling but from what we've seen so far, you are no imposter Diego. I'm impressed with how well you keep your cool under pressure. You've been a Godsend to us."

Callie looked up at Diego then and stared for a long time but said nothing. As if he could feel her stare he looked down at her and winked and she smiled.

Then Shelby noticed Diego watching in the mirror more often. His eyes darted from the road to the GPS to the mirror and her nerves began to stretch tight like a rubber band about to snap.

Checking her mirror on the outside she noticed a black car following them. As they continued down the road she checked her mirror often to see the same car still following. Looking at the GPS she noted that they'd be coming up on a town soon and the car would hopefully pull off in town somewhere.

Inhaling slowly and letting it out at the same speed, she tried calming herself so Callie didn't sense her fear, but Callie was a very bright intuitive girl and looked up at her.

"What's wrong Aunt Shelby?"

Squeezing Callie she plastered a smile on her face. "Nothing sweetie. I just thought that car behind us was following us, but I think it'll turn off in the town we're coming up on."

"How do you know there's a town coming up?"

Pointing to Diego's GPS on his dashboard console she showed Callie the cluster of buildings and roads that merged together in the town. "That there shows us there is a town coming up soon."

The traffic began to increase as they neared the town and Diego put on a turn signal and exited at the first exit. The black car followed and Shelby braved a look at Diego whose nod was almost imperceptible but it was there.

He turned right at the bottom of the exit and the car followed them. Diego's phone rang and he tapped the answer icon.

"Yeah."

"Hey, it's Charly. Why did you turn off?"

"I think we're being followed."

Charly exhaled and he could hear her tapping on her key board. "Okay, get back on the highway and Van and I will come and meet you along the way. I'll also see if I can find a local cop to pull over your tail. Give me a description of the car."

Diego gave Charly a description and Shelby watched in her mirror. Callie began to cry softly next to her and Shelby wrapped her tighter in her arm and tried soothing her.

"It's alright sweetheart, we'll be fine. Did you hear Charly, they're going to come and help us."

Callie only nodded and if she'd been able to turn around in her seat she'd check on Anders. He was quiet in the back. Diego glanced in the backseat and then looked over at her. "He's sleeping."

Nodding her head she was grateful for that at least. He'd not have this fear going through his mind and her not able to comfort him back in the backseat.

Noting a stop light up ahead, Diego muttered under his breath. Then said to Charly, "Stop light."

"Van found a cop on duty. You should be hearing him shortly."

She held her breath and watched the car to make sure no one got out of the car as they slowed. Then, as if they were being watched from above, the light turned green and Diego was able to continue on through the light and exit up on the highway. The black car continued to follow them and it was pretty obvious that the car was indeed following them now. Sirens could be heard in the distance and Diego continued watching things from his vantage point in the mirror and saw the lights moving toward them. "They're coming."

Glancing in her mirror she saw the lights gaining on them and held her breath as they neared. Diego slowed down and the car behind them slowed instead of passing. Then, as it was the law, Diego pulled over to the side of the road, to allow an emergency vehicle or police cruiser to pass, the cruiser passed them and kept going and her heart sank. He wasn't coming to help them.

Her heart beat so fast it hurt in her chest as her eyes darted to the mirror every other second. She'd make herself dizzy at this point.

"Charly, a cop just passed us, any word?"

"That wasn't our cop. Just keep going Diego. By now the car's occupant knows that you suspect him following you."

Just as she said those words the black car hit them from behind. Not hard, but enough to make the average person stop and check out the damage. Diego wasn't the average person though. Hopefully.

Anders woke up and started crying and Callie cried harder. Ted began pacing as much as he could in the back of the car. He'd stick his head out the window then he'd come back in and lick Anders' face. On and on. Then, the black car hit them harder and Diego struggled to keep the truck going straight. She tried swallowing but had difficulty in doing so. Once more, bam, they were hit again.

30

F ighting to keep the truck on the road and going straight he realized the driver of the black car had experience in this sort of action. Hitting them on the edge of either side of the bumper could send the truck spinning.

"Charly..."

"I hear it. Get going. Our cop is on his way right now."

Diego sped up but not so fast that if the car tried hitting them again they'd whip around and hit the ditch. They'd be sitting ducks for sure. Both hands firmly on the steering wheel, he inched the accelerator down and noticed it took the black car a while to speed up to match him. Then he saw the blue and red lights flashing and held his breath this was their guy. The cop pulled in behind the black car with his sirens on and flashing his headlights on and off letting the car know he was expected to stop. Watching and waiting Diego kept his speed even as they continued on and the black car stopped for the cop. As soon as the car stopped he let out his breath.

"Charly, our guy has him. When you come to meet us, bring two car seats with you. One a booster for a 7 year old and one for a 5 year old."

"Got it. Stop at the next town up, Grasshopper Creek, go to the Hotel 84, Room 215 is yours. I've got it booked. We'll see you in about a half hour. Emmy's here now to watch our progress and yours. We're also trying to figure out how they found you again."

Diego nodded. "Exactly what I was wondering."

"Out."

The line went dead and Diego took in a deep breath then let it out.

"Hey there guys, how about we stop and get some ice cream in Grasshopper Creek before we go to our hotel room?"

Anders had stopped crying and through broken breaths said. "I want chocolate."

He smiled, more to reassure Anders but also because the kid was cute. Crying one second, happy to get ice cream the next.

He looked in the mirror at Callie and said, "What do you say Callie? Ice cream?"

"I don't want to get out of the truck."

He nodded. "I understand. We'll go through a drive thru, get our ice cream then head up to the hotel room. My friends wouldn't have booked it if they didn't have a plan."

Callie looked up at him, her eyes red rimmed and shiny. "Okay."

He then looked at Shelby and saw her staring at him. "Why would they want us to go to a hotel?"

"I'm guessing they don't want us bringing them to our compound until we know how they found us again. Somehow they're tracking us. At first we thought it was your vehicle. But, clearly we don't have that now."

"So then how..."

He glanced at her again, her mouth open, her eyes rounded and fear on her face.

"Hey." He said it softly, the GPS telling him to turn off at the next exit. Shelby blinked and he was careful when he spoke. "We'll check it all out, okay?"

She closed her mouth and swiped at her eyes. Then inhaled deeply and let the breath out glancing down at Callie, she faked a smile. "Okay. I wouldn't mind a chocolate cone myself."

Diego turned off the highway, following the instructions the GPS gave him, but as soon as he saw a place that might have ice cream, he'd pull in. It didn't take him long to find a little chain store that sold ice cream and also had a drive-up window. He pulled up to the window and began placing their orders. He looked at Shelby once again, "You want a cone or a cup?"

"Cup. For all of us please."

"Callie, what kind of ice cream do you want?"

"Vanilla."

Looking at the woman taking his order at the window he ordered. "We need three chocolate cones put in cups and two vanilla cones in cups."

He pulled money from his wallet as the woman at the window replied. "That will be $11.58."

Handing her a $20 dollar bill he chuckled when Ted's head lay on his shoulder again. "I got you buddy."

Ted's tail wagged and Anders giggled. That was a great sound to hear.

The woman then came back with a bag and his change. Handing the bag to Shelby he tucked his change into his front pocket, then pulled slowly away from the shop, and began to follow the GPS instructions once again for the hotel.

It wasn't far, the town was fairly small, around fifty thousand people or so, which by most standards was small, but he now lived in Lynyrd Station which was much smaller, around twenty-five thousand people.

Turning into the hotel lot, he looked at Shelby. "Just the bag of ice cream for right now. I'll get Ted's vest on so he will be alright to come in. Just hang tight for a second."

Climbing out of the driver's seat he then opened the back door, pulled Ted's vest from the floor and snapped it on. Grabbing Ted's dishes and cooler, he then hooked the leash to the back of the vest and Ted jumped from the vehicle.

Looking across at Anders he smiled, "You want to help me carry Ted's dishes Anders?"

Anders eagerly nodded and he was happy to see the resilient little guy hang tough under the circumstances. His eyes caught Shelby's over the seat and she nodded and opened her door to get out.

Reaching across the seat he unbuckled Anders seat belt and the little guy scooted over to him and he lifted Anders to the ground, handed him Ted's empty dishes then closed the door, walking alongside Ted and Anders, Shelby and Callie caught up to them and they walked into the hotel together.

Standing at the front desk, he looked at the gentleman behind the desk. "My boss called in a room for me, Room 215."

"Yes, sir. I have it all ready for you."

He scanned the keys and handed them to Diego, who then signed in and they all quietly walked to the elevator to the right of the lobby. Once inside he heard Shelby let out a breath and he felt so danged sorry for her. For all of them actually. She likely never expected any of this to take place.

The elevator stopped on the second floor and they stepped out and into the hall, searching for room 215. Finding it, he handed Shelby one key, then waved the other in front of the door and opened it up. Stepping back, he let Shelby and the kids go in before him. Then he and Ted entered, closed and locked the door, and he let out a sigh.

31

She got the kids settled at the little table in the room with their ice cream and spoons which the ice cream shop had provided. They dug into their treats and she didn't have the heart to tell them she really didn't want hers. Her stomach was twisted into tiny little knots and about a hundred of them at that. If this was Kurtis, and she had no doubt it was, he was ramping up his attacks and by now he'd also know she had help.

It was strange that he hadn't called the police when he found them missing. He'd called RAPTOR. She couldn't help but wonder if he suspected that she'd run or if he'd been planning something closer to home but she'd spoiled his plans and now he had to take it on the road.

Diego took Ted's ice cream and put it in his bowl, then set the bowl on a towel on the floor to protect the carpets. As soon as he took Ted's vest off, the pup lunged at his bowl, making the kids laugh.

Diego smiled at them. "Ted loves ice cream."

Anders agreed. "Me too." And shoveled another spoonful of the chocolate goodness into his mouth.

Diego nodded at her paper bowl and she smiled weakly, but opened the lid and took a small bite. It was wonderful, and had things been different, she'd love spending time with the kids and Diego enjoying ice cream and laughing at Ted.

Diego sat on the bed opposite her and opened his ice cream and scooped some into his mouth.

She locked eyes with him and quietly asked, "How are they tracking us?"

"I suspect your suitcases have tracking devices on them."

Her eyes rounded and she sat straight up. A quick glance showed her the kids were enjoying their desserts and she grabbed the remote for the television off the table between the beds and turned the television on.

"What do you guys want to watch?"

They both yelled out the names of some of their favorite cartoons and she tried finding one they both enjoyed. Settling on one, the kids sat in rapt attention as they ate their ice cream and watched television.

"What's the plan now?" She asked Diego quietly.

Diego looked at her and heaved out a breath. "Once Van and Charly arrive, they'll check the suitcases for the devices. In the meantime, Emmy is likely trying to make contact with Kurtis to find out what he knows. By now, he's on to us and his guy has probably reported back to him that we got away. But the tracking is still in place.

That's why we're at a hotel. It will be difficult for them to know where we are inside here and they can only hope to wait outside. I'm not going out until Van and Charly get here because if someone is watching for me and they hit me, you'll be unprotected. So, for now, we wait."

She let that sink in. She *tried* to let it sink in but honestly, how did you let that kind of information settle?

Setting her ice cream on the table she folded her hands together and slid them between her knees. She fought the urge to curl up into a ball and cry.

"I never dreamed anything like this would happen."

She watched as he licked his lips and her mind sprang instantly to thoughts of a more carnal nature, then she silently scolded herself. But, damn, when he slid his tongue along his lips, he was honest-to-God sexy.

"I'm sure you didn't. For what it's worth, I don't know how you could have expected or guessed any of this."

She nodded her head while she watched his face. "Does your company believe me? Do you believe me that I never meant to hurt the kids?"

His brows rose into the hair that fell over his forehead. Soft whisps of hair that were naturally just there but were supposed to be combed off to the side. Unruly or wild and untamed, much like she'd describe Diego to a girlfriend if asked. He was controlled--he had to be--but there was something so wildly different about him that she found herself trusting him when she didn't even know him. But, they'd spent a night together and he never so much as made her feel like he was dishonest or anything other than a genuine good person. She told him things she'd likely not tell anyone else. And right now, he was the only person standing between Kurtis and her and the kids.

"I believed you right away. If you'd planned on doing them harm, you'd have done it out of the gate, not prolong it. Emmy and the others must believe you too or they wouldn't be trying to circumvent Kurtis' questions about where you are and whether we've made contact, though he likely suspects now."

"Can he sue you or hurt your company?"

Diego shrugged, "He can try. If we're able to collect evidence that he had anything to do with Stacy's disappearance and the hiring of men to harm you and the kids, he won't go very far with it."

She nodded; that was good. "Are you looking for evidence?"

Diego leaned forward. His elbows planted on his knees, but his open hands reached out for hers and she willingly lay her hands in his. The second their skin touched, it was electric. They both felt it, she saw it in his eyes. His thumbs brushed the backs of her hands as he stared into her eyes. "We're looking for everything we can find."

His phone chimed and he squeezed her hands once then let her go, but she could tell he was reluctant to do so. Maybe she hoped he was reluctant to do so.

"Okay."

He pulled his keys from his pocket and held them to his phone, then pushed the unlock button on the key fob.

The male voice on the other end of the phone said, "Got it."

He hung up, then met her gaze. His eyes were beautiful light brown with flecks of darker brown in them. His full lips and clear skin made her envious of his features. "They're here. They're checking out the suitcases now; they won't go rummaging through them, but use a device we have that can locate electronic signals. As soon as we know where the trackers are, they'll let us know."

Just as the words were out of his mouth a series of gun shots sounded from outside.

32

Diego ran to the window as if he could see anything. There was nothing on this side of the hotel. He couldn't leave them and the feeling of helplessness enveloped him. A few more shots sounded and the kids both looked up at him, their eyes round with fear. Callie's lip quivered.

Kneeling in front of the kids, he tried to convey a calm he didn't feel and the reassurance they needed.

"Listen, it'll be okay. My friends are here now and they're helping us. It's so important that you two stay calm and don't scream or make a lot of noise. Okay?"

A lone tear slid unchecked down Callie's cheek.

"You two have been absolute rock stars through all of this but I promise, it won't be long and you'll be safe and playing with other kids who will so enjoy playing with you two."

Shelby stepped forward. "Come and sit with me on the bed. We'll snuggle together until Diego's friends come and tell us we can leave."

Anders scooted from his seat at the table and wrapped his arms around Shelby's leg. His heart broke for these two little kids. They'd been through so much the past month. More than most adults go through in an entire year, and yet they were resilient.

Ted trotted over, still licking his face from remnants of the ice cream he'd slopped over himself. He sat facing Anders, waiting for a sign that all was well.

"Can Ted sit with us too?"

Shelby smiled. "Sure, there's plenty of room."

Anders crawled on the bed then patted it and smiled when Ted climbed up next to him. Anders occupied himself petting Ted as Shelby led Callie to the bed and sat with her back to the headboard. Callie snuggled up alongside her, watching the television as Shelby patted her back.

When Shelby glanced up at him, her expression was sad. He knew she was wrestling with her decision to take the kids away. It wasn't an easy decision she'd made. Either let the children be abused and treated horribly—or worse, "disappeared"—or make herself a criminal and kidnap them to hopefully give them a better life. But, so far they'd dealt with far more than she was equipped to handle and he saw the strain in her now as reality continued to rain hell down on them.

A knock sounded at the door and Diego turned to them with his forefinger held to his lips, a silent plea to be quiet.

He walked to the door, pulled his gun from a holster in his waistband, engaged a bullet into the chamber and looked out the peephole in the door.

Breathing a sigh of relief, he slid the magazine from his gun, then slid the slide on his gun to a closed position before reinserting the magazine. Holstering his weapon, he unlocked the door lock and opened the swing bar security lock. Opening the door he stepped back to let Van into the room. Looking out into the hall he asked, "Where's Charly?"

"Dealing with the shit show downstairs."

Diego tilted his head toward the kids and Van straightened. "Sorry. She's taking care of business."

Reengaging the locks on the door, Diego then stepped past Donovan and into the room.

"So, this is one of my team members, Donovan Keach. We call him Van." He locked eyes with Shelby. "Van, this is Shelby Davidson and Callie and Anders Kennedy."

Van reached forward and shook Shelby's hand then he extended his hand to each of the kids, who in turn shook his hand in return. Van smiled as they did so and Diego couldn't stop feeling pride for these two kids. They were fantastic little humans.

Shelby nodded then her eyes sought his and he felt...his heartbeat increased in a different way than when he was scared. His body felt alive. He wanted to sit next to her to protect her and the kids from everything bad.

Smiling at Shelby to reassure her, his heart sang when she smiled in return.

Ted's head rose and his tail wagged as Van reached over and scratched him behind the ears, but he didn't get up and leave his new post.

"Van, tell us what happened."

Van turned to him, then lowered his voice. "Should we step into the hallway?"

Shelby nodded. Ted's head cocked, but then he lay back down, apparently content to be lying in bed next to Anders and Callie.

Unlocking the door he stepped out and waited as Van followed him pulling the door closed behind him.

"Someone was waiting for you in the parking lot. He drove a black Buick, I think the same one that was following you earlier. It's clear the tracking devices were working. As soon as we opened the truck and scanned the suitcases, he opened fire on us. Luckily Charly was watching and saw him pull his weapon, her vigilance and quick actions saved my ass today. I'll likely never hear the end of it."

Diego smiled knowing Van was right and it felt good not to have a weight pushing down on his chest for a moment.

"We found tracking devices on the kids' suitcases. Nothing on Shelby's."

Diego looked at the door then back at Van. "Kurtis figured Shelby would leave with them?"

Van shrugged.

Then Diego straightened his spine. "Maybe it goes back further. Kurtis was having an affair. Shelby told me. Maybe he thought Stacy was going to leave with the kids so he put trackers on all of their suitcases. Let's identify the tracker system and see if we can figure out if there was one on Stacy's suitcase and track that. We might be able to find out where she went."

"Fuck, Diego, that's a great idea."

Van pulled his phone from his pocket and called headquarters. Maybe they'd be able to solve this whole mess and soon. Sending up a silent prayer that Stacy was still alive, he waited as Van ended his call.

"Okay, Cyber Team is on it. Are you all ready to head to RAPTOR?"

33

S helby's stomach twisted. Not knowing what had happened and what was going to happen was killing her.

"Aunt Shelby?"

She looked down at Callie, whose wide eyes were filled with fear.

"What honey?"

"Are we in trouble?"

"No honey. We're just in a bit of a bind but Diego is helping us out."

"But, why did you take Anders and me away from home? Is it because we were bad like Mommy?"

The door opened and Diego and Van walked into the room but she couldn't get a good read on Diego's mood. He was often like a closed book, the mask he wore to keep everyone out.

Callie looked at Diego. Shelby responded, "Honey, your mommy wasn't bad, she was good. So good."

"That's not what Dad said. He said she was bad. Nosey and a little snoop. And that's why she had to go."

Shelby looked deeply into Callie's eyes. So blue and clear, just like Stacy's. Her dark hair shone in the sunlight from the window but her little forehead wrinkled with worry now.

"When did your father say that sweetheart?"

Callie looked down at her fingers then and Anders started crying. Ted climbed on Anders' lap to comfort him.

Shelby wrapped her left arm around Anders' shoulders and pulled him close to her body. Kissing the top of his head, she just held him. Her right hand sought Callie's hands and she wrapped her fingers around Callie's much smaller hands and softly asked her again. "Callie, sweets, when did your father say your mommy was nosey and snooped and had to go?"

A big tear tracked down Callie's cheek and her sad glistening eyes stared up into her own. Callie replied, "When he pulled her hair and pushed her down the stairs at home. Then he got her suitcase and saw Anders and me standing at the top of the stairs and he told us to go to our room and if we ever said anything about it, we'd end up like her."

Shelby leaned forward slowly and kissed Callie's forehead, then swiped the tear from her cheek with her thumb. Looking Callie in the eye she softly said, "Nothing bad will happen to you. Ever. That's why I took you away from your father. I won't let anything bad happen to you if I can help it. I love you and Anders so much it hurts."

Diego sat on the second bed next to her and Callie and leaned forward much like he had before, with his elbows on his knees. He held his hands out and open, palm up, to Callie, and looked into her eyes. They stared at each other for a long time, so long in fact she didn't know if she should say something, but the look in Diego's eyes was mesmerizing.

Then she saw him swallow and Callie put her hand into Diego's as he softly said to her, "I will help your Aunt Shelby protect you and Anders. You are not in trouble and you didn't do anything wrong. Okay?"

Callie nodded then looked up at Van who stood still as can be watching over them all. "I'll help Diego and your Aunt Shelby and so will Charly."

"I'm Charly."

A blond slender woman with short blond curly hair walked into their room and stood next to Van. She was beautiful with bright blue eyes and perfect teeth, perfect complexion, narrow waist; actually everything was perfect about her, except she was missing an arm. Her left arm was missing from the elbow down, though she had a prosthetic arm that looked fairly real.

She smiled at the kids and they smiled back. She had a vibrancy about her that filled the room with an invisible energy.

Anders looked at her and his brows bunched together. "You're Charly? I thought Charly was a boy like my friend Charlie at school."

Charly laughed and, gosh it was hard not to be jealous of her; she was everything Shelby was not. Light, gorgeous, happy, energetic, carefree.

"My name is Charlesia but everyone calls me Charly."

Callie studied her and a smile formed on her face.

Charly reached forward with her right hand to shake Anders' hand and he shook it.

"What's your name, Love?"

"Anders."

"Ah, Anders, that's a great name."

She shook Callie's hand, "And what is your name?"

"Callie."

"Wow, you all have great names."

She then looked directly at Shelby and smiled. "Hi Shelby, it's nice to finally meet you in person."

"It's nice to meet you too Charly."

Charly sat at the foot of the bed and Ted scooted toward her and she immediately began petting him and scratching behind his ears. Then Ted rolled onto his back and Charly laughed and scratched his belly. His leg started kicking, much to the delight of the kids.

Diego took a deep breath and Shelby looked over at him.

"We can go back to RAPTOR now. Charly and Van will follow us to make sure we don't have any issues."

"Okay." She glanced at Van who still stood close by and then she looked at Charly and smiled.

Diego then said, "If you'd prefer to ride with them you can."

Her head shook of its own doing. "No, I'd like to ride with you."

"The kids can ride with them or us."

"No, the kids stay with me." She snapped. Then realized how desperate that likely sounded and added, "Please."

Diego smiled at her then and she felt better. Actually better than better. Things were finally going to be okay. She felt it in her body. Her heart didn't feel as heavy as it had before. A weight had been lifted.

Diego stood then and she checked that Callie was all right, handed her a tissue from the bedside table and wiped her nose, then looked at Anders who still sat laughing at Ted and staring like a star-struck teen at Charly. Yes, she was that magnetic.

34

The car seats were installed in the truck and both Anders and Callie now sat in the backseat, with Ted sitting behind Diego. Ted needed to stick his head out the window. Anders sat in the middle and Callie behind Shelby. Everyone seemed to feel as though things were different now. Things were better.

They drove in silence for some time when Anders finally asked, "What happened to Charly's arm?"

Diego glanced at Anders in the mirror, "She was shot in the arm. Her bones couldn't be fixed so they had to amputate her arm."

"What's amptate?"

Shelby turned in her seat and looked back at Anders. "Amputate. It means doctors had to cut her arm off to save her life because it was so damaged."

"Oh." Anders thought for a while then asked, "Did it hurt?"

He glanced at Shelby briefly then back to the road. Pushing a couple buttons on his steering wheel the robotic voice asked him what he wanted to do.

"Call Charly."

"Calling Charly on cell."

The sounds of ringing came over the speakers then Charly answered.

"Hey Diego, what's up?"

"Charly, the kids are questioning your arm and trying to understand. Anders asked if it hurt when you had it amputated. Can you explain it to them?"

"Sure. It hurt when it first happened. But I healed up. Sometimes I have phantom pain. That's where it feels like I still have my hand and my fingers itch but they aren't there and there's no way to scratch it. It's weird I guess but I make do. Plus, I have this cool electronic arm now, so it's all good."

He glanced at Anders once again and saw him looking at his own arms.

Then Anders asked, "Can't you scratch your electric arm?"

Charly laughed on the other end of the phone and Diego laughed with her. He glanced at a smiling Shelby. With the pressure of the past few hours lifted, her face changed; it was nice to see. She was a beautiful woman. Inside and outside.

"Of course I can scratch it but I don't have feelings in it because it isn't real. When we get to RAPTOR, I'll let you take a closer look. Deal?"

"Deal."

Then, Anders turned his attention to Ted once more and Diego chuckled. "I guess you answered his questions Charly. See you in a bit."

He ended the call and continued driving. They turned south and the scenery changed to a more picturesque landscape, lush and green. Shelby watched out the windows, a new serene expression on her face.

Finally after a few miles she looked his way. "How long have you all worked together?"

"About a year now. Emersyn Copeland, you'll meet her when we get there, is our boss. She started RAPTOR a year ago. She recruited me, Van, Charly and Creed from the retraining program we were in. The others have come on by different ways, friends of friends mostly. Falcon's father, Ford, works for Emersyn's Uncle Gaige at GHOST and they are all housed next door to us. We work closely with all of them. And Gaige helped Emmy both financially and business-wise get RAPTOR started and set up. GHOST has been around for more than twenty years, so we have the best of the best by way of support and equipment. Plus, when it comes to care and training, we have all that too. You'll meet everyone eventually. GHOST has a resident doctor, Isabella Masters, who is my best friend Josh's wife. We have a resident gun expert who trains with all of us all the time, Bridget Dunbar. It's actually a dream come true to work with these people."

"Wow. I had no idea."

He just smiled. He loved talking about his teammates and all they had at their disposal. Nothing did more for his therapy than this job and association with all of these great people. And he had the support of everyone.

Shelby's voice lowered and she asked, "How did Kurtis know about you?"

He looked at the worry on her face and shrugged. "I don't know. Emmy said word was spreading about us."

But, that was a good question. Up till now, most of their work was referred from GHOST. It worked well as they did similar missions but in different fields. Most recently there had been times when Emmy had been able to refer a couple clients to GHOST which made her feel so good to be able to pay it back. One thing Gaige had always said, "We don't always know how folks find out about us. The people we help know other people and will spread the word that way." So basically don't look a gift horse in the mouth. But, now he was wondering how Kurtis had found out about them and he'd ask Emmy to inquire further, if it mattered.

They drove past the sign for Lynyrd Station and he said, "Only about fifteen minutes now."

They drove past the first exit and took the second one. "We won't go through town right now, but I can take you all out later and show you the town a little if you like. It's small, but it's very nice and the people are friendly."

"That would be wonderful."

Anders asked, "Do you have ice cream here?"

He laughed and so did Shelby. "Yes buddy, we have ice cream."

His eyes continued to shift in Shelby's direction. He liked a lot about her. From all he knew about her from this terrible experience, she was amazing. Imagine what she'd be like when the pressure was off. Imagine all that could be when life was good for them all.

Inhaling deeply and letting it out he reminded himself not to get too caught up in dreaming about anything. Once they figured out what was up with Kurtis, Shelby and the kids would no doubt go back home and he wouldn't see them again.

That thought sat very heavy in his heart as he turned on his right signal to turn into the driveway of RAPTOR Headquarters and his home.

35

S helby took in the grounds that were RAPTOR. The old southern mansion across the lawn was where GHOST lived and worked according to Diego.

The pride in his voice was evident as he explained their new home away from home.

"This building, while not as elaborate as the GHOST mansion, is brand new and efficient for us. Since Emmy just started this business and we needed to spend money on the equipment we need and then to have a place for us to live and be safe, our money went to efficiency versus outward appearances. That's not to say GHOST is all about appearances, but when they came here to Indiana, they had been established already. They wanted to fit in and that old home was here, so Gaige had it retrofitted to their needs. But, wait till you see the inside of RAPTOR, it's amazing."

She smiled as he almost apologized that this wasn't a mansion he was bringing them to. "Diego, you don't need to be apologetic about this building, it's beautiful."

It was, too. All tumbled brick with some detailing here and there, it wasn't a square building that looked like a prison; it was styled in a modern form, yet neat and clean.

Diego chuckled. "You're right. And I'm sorry if I made it seem as though I was apologizing. We have a wonderful place here and I'm excited for you to see it inside."

"We're looking forward to seeing it. Actually, a shower and the ability to actually lay down and sleep without worry sounds like a slice of heaven."

Diego pushed a button and the garage door at the back of the building opened up. As he pulled in she saw the light, clean garage, highly organized and neat.

"I agree with you there."

Pulling into an empty spot in the garage, she noticed a logo on the wall in front of his truck, which was a shield outlined in orange with an angular wolf on it and Team Alpha written on the top.

"Team Alpha?"

He smiled. "We're split up loosely into three teams. Van, Charly and I are Team Alpha. We mostly handle all recon and recovery. Then we have Team Bravo which are Piper, Caiden and Deacon and they are our Cyber team. Their computer skills are nuts. And Team Charlie is Falcon, Creed and Emmy and they are our special ops team. They're the team that most resembles and works with GHOST."

"Wow, that sounds highly organized."

He chuckled. "It's organized and Emmy has done a terrific job in matching us with our specialties and teaming us up. It doesn't mean we don't work with the other teams. Obviously, Cyber team has been helping us with this mission."

His choice of words brought her back to reality. She had to remember they were a mission to Diego. It didn't matter that she found him attractive and magnetic, he was doing his job and she'd do well to remember that hero worship or protector love would only get her heart broken.

"It all works. Are you all ready to go in and meet everyone?"

Shelby looked into Diego's eyes. "What are the chances we could clean up before meeting everyone?"

He smiled at her and nodded. "I think those are pretty good chances. Give me a second."

He pulled his phone off the dashboard holder and typed something out. A few seconds later a reply came back and he read it out loud. "Emmy says you'll be in the room next to mine; it's all set up for you. Shioban has toiletries and clean towels and linens in the room and Sheldon will have dinner ready in an hour."

"Who are Shioban and Sheldon?" It was going to be hard for her to keep everyone straight. She could do it though.

He laughed then and, oh goodness, it looked so good on him. His eyes actually sparkled. "Shioban is our house-keeper. She keeps us neat and orderly and she's also a bit of a sass. She doesn't let us get away with much. She's first generation Irish-American and her brogue is strong but cute. Sheldon is our chef. Former military and if you have a secret, it will go to his grave with him if you see fit to share it with him. He's usually not all that talkative, but he has a way with a stove and oven and he keeps us fed well."

"I have to go potty." Anders said from the backseat and she giggled. There were more important things going on here besides her embarrassment if she forgot someone's name.

"Okay, buddy, let's go inside."

She opened her door and stepped out as Diego did the same before helping Ted and the kids out of the truck. Diego then pulled the cooler from the back. Van and Charly parked their vehicle and pulled their suitcases from the back of their SUV. That's when she wondered if she'd ever get her vehicle back. She was a kidnapper now and they'd likely not give it back to her until this was all settled. Oh, so much was happening so quickly.

"Hey there Anders, are you ready to meet everyone?" Charly asked as she approached.

"I have to go potty," he repeated.

Diego chuckled. "I'm taking them up to their room first to use the bathroom and clean up, then we'll come down and meet everyone."

"Sounds like a plan." Charly took Callie's suitcase from Van and pulled both kids' bags as Van handed Diego Shelby's suitcase.

Ted followed alongside Diego, he knew the routine by now.

Charly waved her card in front of the elevator and the doors opened. She stepped in and waited for the rest of them to step in with her. Anders stood next to her looking at her prosthetic arm. Charly smiled at him. "Go ahead and touch it."

His eyes rounded as he looked at her and she smiled. His fingers reached out tentatively and touched her left arm and his face scrunched up.

"It's cold."

"Yes, usually. It isn't real so it doesn't heat or cool like our bodies do."

Callie stared at it and touched it too. Her fingers smoothed up and down the side of it. "It's soft though."

Charly smiled and so did Shelby. Callie wanted to be nice about it. She was such a sweet girl.

The elevator doors opened and one by one they stepped out into the hall on the second floor. Van turned to Diego and Shelby.

"Once you've had a chance to unpack, we'd like to see the suitcases. We've managed to disable the trackers, but we'd like to pull them out and see if we can get the actual information on them and see if there was a tracker on Stacy's suitcase. These will help us with that."

Nodding her head, she smiled at him. "I'll unpack right away and bring them to you. Thank you."

36

Diego took a shower then headed downstairs to see what Team Bravo was able to find out about the trackers. He also wanted to get Shelby a cell phone to use.

He stepped off the elevator with a spring in his step, he realized with a grin. Being home had some healing powers, that was a fact. And there was no doubt this was home.

The activity inside the operations center invigorated him. Piper manned the computers. Her short blond hair, always neatly arranged in some fashion, was pulled into a ponytail at the back of her head.

"Hey Diego, how are Shelby and the kids?"

"They're cleaning up and getting ready to meet everyone."

"Where's Ted?"

"Keeping the kids occupied and enjoying every minute of it."

These were the questions you asked a man about his family and he answered them so easily. The fact that he also enjoyed answering them gave him pause, so he changed the subject.

"What are you working on?"

"I'm looking at the trackers on the kids' suitcases and I've found the company and the vendor who sold them to Kennedy. Those are tracked by serial number and..." She looked closely at the screen then clicked her mouse a couple of times, "and I just found another one purchased by Kurtis Kennedy and believe that one is on Stacy's suitcase."

He leaned in and looked at her computer screen, "Are you able to ping it to see if it's active?"

Piper tapped a few keys on her computer, turned up the volume and clicked her mouse a few times. He held his breath as they waited for the signal. Sometimes the truth was worse than the fiction and at this point, the kids believed their mom had to go away because she was bad. But, if she were dead and their father killed her, that would be a horrible finality they'd have to live with the rest of their lives.

Taking a deep breath, Diego watched Piper's computer screen, but he wasn't sure if he was waiting for a visual indication or an audio one. He was just about to ask when a small red dot flashed on the screen.

Piper instantly zoomed in on the red dot and waited. It took a few seconds but it blinked once more. Zooming in closer, she tried again, her actions growing more excited as she zeroed in on the tiny red dot. Another flash from the dot and she highlighted the area on her computer screen again.

Van and Charly walked into the room at that time and stood silently watching what Piper was doing.

Piper blew up the area she'd isolated, moved it to the monitor next to her and filled the screen with her finding.

"It's here. The location will populate on the screen in a minute but the third tracker that Kurtis Kennedy purchased is here. The signal is beginning to fade though.

A few seconds later the location coordinates appeared on the screen. Piper did a geolocation on the coordinates: Fallsville, Kansas, just ninety minutes from the Kennedy home. "Who wants this? I'll send the exact location to your GPS."

Charly and Van both responded. "I'll go."

Charly then looked at Diego. "You really should stay here with them and get them settled in."

Diego nodded; she was right.

"Okay, I just sent it off to both of your GPS's. Stay in touch."

Charly and Van both waved and immediately left the room. Diego watched after them, torn about staying or going, but staying was the right thing. The kids had been through enough in the past few days. Shelby had too.

"Thank you Piper. I also need a phone for Shelby to use. She only has a burner right now."

"Okay, give me a few minutes and I'll have one ready for her."

"Thanks." He went to his desk on the opposite side of the conference table from Cyber's computers. He looked over the paperwork and the file on Shelby and the kids to re-familiarize himself with the details. First of all, why would Kurtis risk the kids seeing him harm Stacy? Eventually, even if he threatened them, which he'd done, they would say something to someone. Unless he thought he wouldn't need them to keep the secret very long?

SmartTech, Kennedy's company, worked in the field of technology as a manufacturer of small components for motherboards and other devices that were then put into computers. He'd grown from a fledgling company just ten years ago to close to a billion dollars today, an extreme growth trajectory. He'd managed to wrangle very high-powered companies as clients in a short amount of time.

Of course, this file didn't mention a mistress. Opening his laptop, he began adding into the electronic file notes what he'd learned from Shelby and the kids. Eventually, their computer program would be able to find matching data from what Kennedy had told them, to the facts as found, to the information Shelby and the kids gave them. The truth always lay somewhere in the middle.

"Diego, I have your phone for Shelby." Piper called from across the room. He finished up his notes and closed his laptop and the file on his desk.

"All here and I have all of our numbers programmed into the phone."

"Thanks Piper. See you at dinner."

He left the conference room and waved his card at the elevator. He waved his card again, impatient to see Shelby and the kids. As he pushed the number 2 and the doors closed again, he shook his head, reminding himself that he needed to keep things in perspective.

Upon landing on the second floor he walked to the left, past the white wooden bench against the wall next to his apartment and to the apartment next door. Ted barked at his knock and he heard the kids laughing. Shelby opened the door and what greeted him made his heart beat furiously in his chest.

37

Her pulse accelerated as she looked at Diego standing in her doorway. Handsome. Oh my he was handsome. Clean shaven except for the Van Dyke he wore which totally worked on him. His fresh scent floated to her and wrapped around her like a warm blanket. The reaction from her body was one hundred percent. There wasn't a cell in her that didn't have a response to him.

"I brought you a cell phone and thought I'd take you on a tour to show you where everything is and introduce you to my teammates."

Her cheeks flushed and burned and her mouth went dry. She stared into his eyes for some time until Ted burst through the door and jumped up on Diego. As if his presence hadn't affected her before, the way he knelt down and smiled while petting his dog and accepting kisses from Ted, well that right there...wow.

Anders walked out to the hall then, giggling at Ted's exuberance. The way Diego looked at Anders and smiled at him, that could have melted the coldest heart.

"Thank you for taking good care of Ted for me. I appreciate it."

Anders nodded. "You take care of me and I take care of Ted."

Diego froze his petting of Ted and stared at Anders. His eyes actually teared up. Then Anders smiled. Diego inhaled and exhaled quickly and Anders lunged forward and hugged Diego.

Oh, be still her heart when Diego wrapped his arms around Anders and a tear slid down his cheek. Her eyes welled instantly with tears and her nose tingled. Callie stepped next to her and wrapped her little arms around Shelby's waist and her tears fell too. These two small children, such good and sweet kids, needed love. They needed to know they were loved. They were starved for it. And scared too. Then guilt washed over her because she'd likely done a poor job of conveying how much she loved them these past days. So nervous about what she'd done and so worried they'd be found that she'd forgotten to hold them close and tell them she loved them so much. She wouldn't make that mistake again.

Finally, Diego stood with Anders in his arms and looked over at her. With a forefinger, he quickly brushed the tears off his cheeks and nodded to her. "Ready?"

All she could do was nod. He turned toward the elevator, but stopped and pulled a cell phone from his back pocket.

"This is for you. Piper programmed all of our numbers into it so if you need someone, you can call us."

She managed to whisper, "Thank you."

He smiled then looked down at Callie. "What do you want to see first, the kitchen, the conference room or our workout room?"

Callie smiled. "The workout room!"

He looked at Anders who nodded and Diego started toward the elevator. "The workout room it is. I'll warn you though, sometimes if a lot of us have been in there working out, it can smell."

"Eww." Callie squealed.

Anders laughed. "I hope it smells."

He led them to the elevator and waved his card in front of the electronic monitor; the doors instantly slid open and he stepped aside to let Shelby and Callie enter first. Then he said to Anders, "A gentleman always lets ladies enter first."

"Okay."

They stepped on then and Shelby couldn't stop looking at the pair. Diego looked wonderful with Anders in his arms. Diego looked happy and alive or excited for the first time since she'd met him. He liked being here.

The elevator doors opened on the lower level and they stepped out. He set Anders on his feet, then took his hand. "So this is where all of our work happens." He turned to the left and pointed. "Down there is our gun range. Sometimes, depending on what we're shooting, you'll hear it, most times not too much."

Turning directly in front of the elevator doors, he held his hand out. "This is our small medical clinic. If we need anything other than basic care, GHOST next door has a larger clinic and Dr. Masters is the resident doctor over there. She's also started a small practice in town. Wyatt, whom you'll meet later, is also a medic so if Isabella, Dr. Masters, isn't available, Wyatt can pitch in."

Turning to the right and down the hall he pointed to two doors. "The door on the right here is our headquarters, we'll go in there in a minute and across from that is the workout room."

She tried remembering everything he told her but she'd likely have to ask him again; there was so much going on at one time and she was struggling to process everything. Plus the over-reaching question that kept flooding her mind was, "What next?"

He walked them to the workout room and opened the door. To her relief it didn't smell too bad, perhaps a bit sweaty. There was a myriad of workout equipment and weights plus some medical looking machinery. She stared at it trying to figure it out.

"As I mentioned before, all of us are wounded veterans. Some of us have more physical or pronounced wounds than others. You met Charly, we also have team members with lung damage and varying degrees of shrapnel, multiple surgeries and pins holding things together. Some of their workouts are modified to their needs. Isabella prescribes the workouts and physical therapy needed, and sometimes, we get injured on our missions."

The realization of all they put themselves through to help others grew her admiration ten-fold for each and every one of them. The kids walked around and looked at the weights and the medicine balls and tried playing with them. The larger equipment offered them a jungle-gym type experience. While they played, he turned to her.

"We found another tracker. Van and Charly went to see what it's attached to. It could be a suitcase, but maybe Stacy is with the suitcase. Don't get your hopes up too high though. Kurtis doesn't seem like a stupid man and if he ki...hurt her, he would be stupid to put a tracker on her."

"Why would he put trackers on the kids' suitcases and why wouldn't he tell you about them?"

He nodded and she watched his eyes dart to the children then land on her again. They were beautiful eyes. "I'm thinking that calling us in was a red herring. He wanted someone to think he was worried about you all while at the same time, hiring someone to kill you. And, why he didn't just call the police makes me believe he has already paid the police off and they can't be pushed much further. You're asking too many questions and in his way. The kids..." He swallowed and she knew he hated saying anything. "I think we know he didn't want them in the first place."

She swallowed the lump in her throat and turned to look at Callie and Anders. Such beautiful children and so much life ahead of them. They'd already endured far more than so many people would have to in a lifetime.

Diego's phone chimed and he looked at the readout.

38

He looked up at Shelby. "I'm sorry to lay all that on you, but I don't want to hide anything from you.

Maybe since you already decided to take the kids and run, you should at least know what you're up against. Emmy said she'll speak with you after dinner to discuss Kurtis, what you can tell her about him and what you know about Stacy's disappearance. I've already updated my notes into the file."

She nodded and smiled at him. It was a soft smile but it was sweet. "Thank you."

When he gazed into her eyes he saw her. She returned his gaze without wavering and he knew, he just knew that she was good. Now he just had to prove it. He took her hand in his and squeezed it.

"You're welcome."

He turned to the kids. "Who's hungry?"

"I am." Anders squealed.

Callie ran toward him. "Me too."

"Okay, let's go see what Sheldon has for us to eat tonight."

"Why do you call him Sheldon?" Anders asked.

Diego laughed. "That's his name bud."

Anders giggled. "It's kind of funny."

"I'll let you in on a secret, don't tell him that or you'll be in the kitchen peeling potatoes for the next year."

Anders looked up at him with solemn eyes and slowly shook his head. "I don't know how."

Instantly sorry he tried to tease him, Diego bent down and scooped Anders into his arms and began walking to the elevator.

"Then let's not say anything about his name and you won't even have to learn."

He tickled Anders and his giggle made everything instantly better.

They entered the elevator and Callie asked to push the button. Diego nodded. "Push the number 1."

Eagerly she pushed the button. The elevator doors began to close when they heard, "Hold up please."

Diego reached out and held the doors open. Piper limped toward the door, and with a smile said, "Thank you."

"Piper, I'd like to introduce you to Shelby Davidson, Callie and Anders Kennedy. This is Piper, she works on Team Bravo as a cyber specialist."

Callie looked up at her. "What's cyber special?"

Piper smiled at her, "Cyber means the internet and electronics. I'm pretty darned good at it too. I can hack a computer, rework a phone, locate anything on the internet and remove things from the internet too. I can also do a bunch of other fun things."

"Do you play computer games?"

Piper laughed. "I've been known to play some games. What do you like to play?"

The elevator doors opened and Piper and Callie stepped off the elevator. Anders squirmed to catch up to them so Diego set him down to run. He looked at Shelby and gestured, "After you."

She blushed and the pink tint in her cheeks beguiled him. He stepped off the elevator behind her and caught up in two strides to walk beside her to the dining room.

A few of his teammates stood around chatting, a few sat at the table, and there were some not in attendance.

He cleared his throat. "Everyone, I'd like you to meet Shelby Davidson, Callie and Anders Kennedy.

There were murmurings of greetings and Diego found them room at the table together. Callie opted to sit next to Piper, who smiled sweetly at her and chatted about video games and cheat codes. Since they were easily found on the internet, there was really no harm in chatting about them. He chuckled as he held Shelby's chair out for her to sit. Anders sat to his left, Shelby to his right.

Sheldon walked out of the kitchen with platters of food and began handing them down the table. Tonight's menu was baked chicken with asparagus and squash. Anders scrunched up his face and Sheldon stopped and looked at him.

"You don't like your vegetables little man?"

Anders looked up at Sheldon, his eyes round as could be and maybe a bit of fear on his face.

"How do you expect to grow up big and strong if you don't eat your vegetables?"

Anders held up his right arm and curled it at the elbow. "I'm already strong."

The snickers around the table told him his teammates were enjoying this exchange.

"Yeah? How strong are you?"

Anders thought for a moment, his brows pinched together, then he said, "I can pick up Callie."

"Sure, sure, but can you pick up Piper?"

Anders eyes grew a smidge larger as he turned his head to look at Piper.

Shaking his head he whispered, "No."

Sheldon laughed then. "Eat your vegetables buddy, that will help. Then, when you've eaten a good dinner, come in the kitchen, I'll have a dessert for you."

Anders smiled from ear to ear but before Sheldon turned to leave the room for more food he looked at Callie and winked, "You too little one."

The asparagus was passed to Diego and he turned to look at Anders, "You gonna try this?"

Anders nodded, "But maybe just a little bit."

Diego laughed. "Deal."

Laying three asparagus stems on his plate, he added some to his own and passed the dish to Shelby. Their fingers touched and his heartbeat quickened. Yeah, something was going on here. The sparkle in her gorgeous green eyes and the soft smile on her lips made him swallow the moisture that gathered in his mouth.

Soon he was passed the squash and he repeated his conversation with Anders, who like a trooper decided to try just a little bit. That kid! He was precious.

This time as he passed the squash to Shelby he looked forward to their fingers touching. He wasn't disappointed.

His phone buzzed with a text at the same time as Emmy's. Both of them looked at their screens and his first response was to look across the table at Emmy.

The slight frown on her gorgeous face told him she was more and more convinced that Stacy's life had terminated, but they still didn't have proof of it. But this was not good news at all.

39

She turned her head. Diego was still looking at Emersyn. Neither of them was smiling. Actually they both looked sad or worried and she began to get that dreaded feeling in the pit of her stomach.

Finally, Diego glanced over at her and whispered, "After dinner let's see if Piper or someone can take the kids for a bit. I can call Sophie or Wyatt from next door and they can come over. Both of them have kids so Callie and Anders can play with them."

"Is everything okay?"

"I'm not sure Shelby, we only briefly got some intel but we'll call in to Charly and Van and see what they've found."

"Okay."

She picked at her food, mostly she moved her food around her plate. She hadn't eaten much in the past few days but the thought of food right now wasn't appealing at all.

Diego texted someone while they ate, and as soon as he received a reply he said to her, "Sophie is home and said to bring the kids over. She has a little boy, Tate, who is just over a year old now. But, she set up a little gym area in the workout room over there and you can meet whoever is over there now."

"Okay. That's very sweet of her."

He chuckled. "Everyone here is super and frankly the way this all works is we're a team. All of us. So, when someone needs something, there's always someone to help out."

"That's wonderful."

She listened to everyone chatting with each other and specifically tuned her ears to both kids chatting away with those on either side of them. She felt weird being here. They all likely thought she was a criminal, and she was. Officially now she was a kidnapper, but if she were arrested, her court record wouldn't say that their father was abusing them and she feared for their lives.

Diego nudged her with his elbow, "Hey, you all right?"

She lay her fork on her plate and straightened her spine. "My stomach is in knots and I'm feeling rather sheepish being here. Everyone here is good and law abiding and helping people."

Diego set his fork down and pushed his plate away from him. He turned slightly in his chair to face her and his eyes grew intense as he stared into her eyes. "What do you think you did?"

"I took the kids. They aren't mine, but I feel like they are. But, the law…"

He took a deep breath, "It's a little late to worry about the law and you did what you did for the right reasons. It may have been impulsive and not completely thought out, but you did it because they are your heart."

"Yes."

He nodded. "Then how are you any different than any of us?"

She stared into his beautiful eyes. Not just the light brown color with the full thick lashes and not the shape of them. But what she saw in them. As in, into his soul or his mind. He was honest and true and he wasn't hiding anything from her. You could tell when someone was lying to you; they weren't able to hold eye contact for very long. He held. For a long time.

She softly smiled and he smiled too. "See, that's it."

"I'm done can I go play?" Anders tugged at Diego's shirt and Diego laughed.

"Yep. We're going to walk next door to meet Sophie and her little boy Tate. They have a playground set up over there and Sophie invited us to go over. How about that?"

"Yes."

Shelby looked at Callie who nodded her agreement in going somewhere to play and Diego pushed his chair back from the table. "We all have to pick up after ourselves. So put your silverware on your plate and take your plate to the kitchen."

He stood and did as he said to do, and she watched with pride as Callie and Anders both followed behind him, each of them carrying their plates with their silverware sliding around on top. Doing the same, she looked across the table to Emmy and said, "Thank you."

"Diego will bring you downstairs when you get back and I'll go over what we have so far."

Tears sprang to her eyes. It was stupid to be this emotional, she didn't even know what they knew. But the looks on their faces earlier told her something wasn't right and she battled with wanting to know and not wanting to know. She felt like a hormonal teenager again bouncing back and forth on the emotional roller coaster of puberty. She didn't care to go back and relive that time in her life, so she needed to get a good handle on herself.

Setting her plate on the rack with the others, she smiled up at Sheldon as he handed each of the kids a cookie, fresh and hot from the oven and wrapped in wax paper so they didn't get all gooey. She then reminded the kids, "What do you say?"

"Thank you." They said in unison and she smiled. "Thank you Sheldon, dinner was delicious."

"You could have fooled me, you ate like a bird."

Her cheeks burned. She didn't realize he was paying attention. She lay her right hand over her stomach as she replied, "It's not that it wasn't good. It was, I'm just a bit tied up inside over..." She looked at the kids. "Events."

"Okay. You get a pass this time. Get your stomach right by morning. And if you can't, come down and see me and I'll set you right."

He turned then and loaded one of the two dishwashers in the kitchen with their dirty plates and she followed Diego and the kids from the kitchen.

"We can walk out the back door here to Sophie's."

He led them down a short hall, which separated the kitchen and the living room, to the back door, opened it and let her pass through. Anders started walking through in front of Callie but Diego halted him. "Anders, ladies first bud."

Anders smiled, chocolate already smeared on his face. "Sorry." He stepped aside to let Callie pass by then Diego nodded at him. "Nice job."

40

H e pulled a chair out for Shelby to sit in at the conference room table. She smiled at him but it didn't reach her eyes. She was nervous and he couldn't blame her. They didn't have great news.

Emmy came to the table and sat across from Shelby; he sat to her right.

"Van and Charly found Stacy's suitcase. They are working with local PD right now to see what else can be found at the scene and have the evidence catalogued. What I've been told so far is that the suitcase was full, stuffed with clothing, haphazardly tossed in without a care. As you told Diego, no undergarments were found and only one pair of shoes, which were sneakers, but the clothing in the suitcase was dresses, cocktail and spring dresses, and dress slacks. Not clothing you'd wear with sneakers. On top of that, no sign of Stacy. So, who would pack a suitcase, then toss it in a dried creek bed?"

Shelby shook her head. "There's absolutely no trace of her anywhere around there?"

"No. I'm afraid not. But police and Charly and Van are looking."

Shelby nodded, then looked up at Emmy. "Isn't it stupid for Kurtis to put a tracker on Stacy's suitcase and then ditch it with the tracker on it? I don't understand."

Diego took a deep breath. "What the kids told us is Kurtis pulled Stacy's hair and tossed her down the stairs. Then he ran up to get a suitcase and forbade them to go down to her. We don't know if she was still alive after he tossed her down the stairs, or if she had been knocked out. We don't know what happened after that. But, Shelby, does he have cameras on the house?"

"Yes. But you know he erased those if they showed anything."

"Right, he lives in a posh neighborhood, so are there other security cameras in the area? How about the neighbors with doorbell cameras or other security devices?"

She straightened up. "That's a high probability. Everyone was all about staying safe there. The neighbor across the street for sure has a doorbell cam. But if Kurtis suspects that you're talking to his neighbors, he'll shut that down."

Emmy leaned forward, "We don't have to talk to the neighbors, we can have Cyber see if they can find the cameras and log into their systems to see any stored videos in the cloud."

"You mean hack..."

"We don't really use that term." Emmy smiled at her and Shelby smiled back.

Nodding, she said, "All I want is to know what happened to my sister and to keep her kids safe from that asshole."

Diego smiled and patted her on the back, "Then let's find out what happened and keep them safe."

Shelby nodded and looked into his eyes. "Yeah, that's good. Thank you."

He needed to kiss her soon. She looked at him like he meant something to her. She'd grown on him in the past couple of days. He genuinely liked her, Shelby the person. And the kids, wow, the kids were so special.

"Okay, so Shelby, let's start at the beginning and get down anything you remember about the last time you saw Stacy. From there, we'll figure out how we can locate where she went."

He watched as she answered their questions. He believed her, every word. She never faltered or fumbled. She remembered it as if it was yesterday and everything she'd told him, she told Emmy. She cried a few times; she cried when she told them of seeing the bruises on Callie and Anders for the first time. She cried when recounting Stacy telling her that Kurtis was having an affair. Her sister was smart and resourceful and Shelby couldn't understand why she'd stay. But, an hour and a half later, she was cried out and Emmy had the full story.

"Much of what you've told me is the opposite of what Kurtis told me. The difference is, Shelby, I believe you, I didn't believe him."

"I have facial recognition." Caiden Marx, one of Team Bravo called out.

Emmy stood and waved Shelby over to the computers. Caiden tapped a few keys and a large screen pulled down from the ceiling in behind his computer on the large wall. Soon his computer screen projected images and Shelby gasped.

"That's Stacy."

"You're sure?" Caiden asked.

"I'm positive." Stacy Kennedy looked very much like Shelby. Dark hair, though Stacy's was long and wavy, and Stacy was a bit fuller figured. Both women were beautiful and the smile on Stacy's face in some of the photos was stunning. She was confident, smart and a woman who knew what she was doing. At least that's the vibe her pictures sent off.

Caiden then tapped his keys. "So, using this facial recognition, I can run these photos through the internet and trace where Stacy was and possibly is now."

Then the pictures vanished and potential matches shuffled through the program with dizzying speed.

Shelby clutched her hands together in front of her and he felt sorry for her, but as always, stood in amazement at the technology that made their lives and jobs so much easier. How did they do it fifty years ago?

Then Stacy's face slowly populated the screen again, and locations were typed under each picture along with the date and time the cameras saw her.

"So, with the increased interest in security cameras, and most larger and even some smaller businesses able to afford cameras, most of them have cloud storage. This is private information but we have some fun software that allows us to peek under the hood for a few things." Caiden explained proudly. "Pictures of people is one of them, based on laws passed in Congress during our former president's administration. If you're in public, you should assume you are on camera somewhere. Then, there's social media, selfies, dating sites, and sadly porn sites, and we can locate a vast majority of people."

The screen filled and Caiden clicked on the first picture. "I have them sorting by date, so oldest to newest. This one is ten years old. Let's find something more recent." He scrolled slowly through the pictures.

Diego saw a date. "There, that one is two days before she disappeared."

Caiden clicked on it and it showed Stacy entering a bank in Kansas City.

"Mark that please." Diego asked. Now they were getting into his specialty area.

The next photo showed Stacy leaving the bank, the time stamp on it was twenty-five minutes later.

"Go back, Caiden." In the first photo, Stacy carried a manilla envelope in her hand. "Now go to the one showing her leaving."

"No envelope. She left it there. Is there a way to zoom in on it?"

Caiden tried but there was no writing on the outside of the envelope.

He turned to Emmy. "We need to find out if Stacy had a safety deposit box in that bank."

41

She tucked the kids into bed, told them their stories of super hero Callie and super hero Anders, and they giggled but fell asleep happy and tired. She had claimed the sofa to sleep on, though Shioban had sweetly offered to bring her a bed while they were here, but she could crawl in with the kids if she needed more room. She was content to sleep across the room where her tossing and turning wouldn't wake them.

She sat on the sofa, depleted after all she'd been through today, when she heard a light knock on the door.

Hefting her tired body from her spot, she padded to the door to see Diego standing there. The instant the door opened, he leaned in and kissed her.

His lips felt soft and full against hers, his warmth seeped into her and his tongue tasted sweet. He'd just eaten a cookie. Pulling back slightly, he searched her eyes for a reaction and her cheeks heated.

"I've wanted to do that for a while now," he whispered.

"I did too." She smiled.

He nodded once then said, "Do you want a drink? Or coffee, tea, warm milk or nothing at all?"

She giggled under her breath. "A beer sounds heavenly."

He grinned. "Your place or mine?"

She looked back at the kids, "If they wake up they'll be worried."

Shaking his head, he stepped back. "Leave the door slightly ajar." Then he pointed to the floor. He'd placed footprints cut out of paper from her door to his. "We'll leave my door open so they can find us."

Her hand flew to her heart and tears welled in her eyes. "That's seriously the most thoughtful thing I've ever seen."

Diego smiled and looked as though he simply enjoyed praise from her.

Shelby stepped out of her apartment, leaving the door ajar, and followed the footsteps next door to Diego's apartment. The rest of the building was nicely decorated, including her rooms, but his wasn't at all. It was clean but plain.

"Why isn't this room decorated?"

His cheeks turned a brilliant shade of pink and she thought it was adorable, even sexy on him.

"I don't know how. And, I haven't had time."

Nodding, she looked around at the room. It wouldn't take much to make this feel more like a home. His home. He deserved that, didn't he? She felt he did. Back in the day, she'd started school to be an interior designer, but once she married, her husband wanted her to stay home and get ready to have children. They tried and tried until years later, she'd learned she couldn't have children. That ended her marriage and she was left with nothing. so she applied for and got a job in a daycare, which she loved.

"Take a seat." He motioned to the sofa across the room. He had nice furniture. Brown leather reclining sofa and love seat with matching tables on both sides of the sofa. On one of the tables were gun and shooting magazines, on the other table he had a book.

She picked up the book and looked at the title, *Valor*.

"What do you like to read?"

He pulled two beers from a small refrigerator and walked toward her.

"True stories, mostly stories of men and women who have fought in the armed forces and won."

"Doesn't that make your PTSD come back to you?"

"Not really. Sometimes, if the writer is very good at describing what's happening, I have to get up and go for a walk because I can feel some of the stirrings of an episode coming on. Mostly, Ted can sense them first and will give me a bit of a nudge."

She looked around for Ted and he chuckled. "The kids wore him out, in a good way, and he's laying in the bedroom on his bed."

She took a deep breath, and let it out slowly before changing the subject. "Do you think Stacy's alive?"

He locked eyes with her and she saw sadness. They changed as he looked at her and she knew he was trying to figure out the best way to say it. She appreciated his candor and she appreciated his gentleness in telling her what she already suspected was the truth.

"It's looking more and more doubtful Shelby. But, wherever she is, alive or not, we'll find her so you all have closure. And if she isn't alive, it's more important to find her to find out who the killer is among you."

"If she isn't, I already know who the killer is. I just don't know why."

He took a drink from his beer then inhaled deeply. "You said they weren't happy and she didn't want to leave him because she wanted him to suffer. What do you think that meant?"

She cocked her head as she thought about that. "Initially I thought she refused to leave because it would be too easy for him. You know, give him a divorce and if she left with the kids, she'd already be out of the house and need to find a place to live. She had no job, and until the court ordered him to pay her support she'd have no money. But, I've been running some of our conversations through my head and some things do seem strange."

"Like what?"

"Like, when she was at that bank? I was babysitting. She told me she was having her hair done. And I remember her leaving that day. I remember her running up to her bedroom to get that envelope and I asked her what was so important that she needed that? She told me it was security. Then she winked at me and slipped out the door.

When she came back, I'd forgotten to ask her what she meant about it and to be honest, my assumption was that she had proof of Kurtis' affair."

He nodded and reached out his left hand to her. Laying her right hand in his she stared at their fingers.

"How would she have gotten proof? Did she hire a private investigator? That's someone we could question."

"She never mentioned anything."

"Okay. If she had a safe deposit box in that bank, who would she tell?"

"Me. But she didn't say anything. And since the facial recognition doesn't show anything after her leaving the bank, then going to the post office, I can't imagine where she'd have gotten any further information to send him into a rage."

He nodded and she saw his mind working. Just the way he looked across the room at nothing, the way his facial expression changed, he was a thinker. God, she loved a thinking man.

42

D iego's phone chimed a text. Pulling his phone up, he glanced at the text from Emmy, then sent a message to her.

He turned his head to Shelby; her gorgeous green eyes looked at him expectantly and a dark dread filled his stomach.

"Emmy's on her way up here."

"Okay. Am I not allowed in here or something?"

He chuckled. "Honey, it's nothing like that and we can have whoever we want in our rooms whenever we want, this is my home. That said, we don't bring strangers here, security and all. But," He twisted to look straight at her and his voice dropped. "I suspect this isn't good news."

He watched her swallow. Her eyes rounded and her jaw tightened. Even with her face filled with fear and dread, she was a beauty. He'd do anything to spare her and the kids further heartache, but it wasn't in his power to do so.

All he could do was be there for them and help make sure justice was served. That, he could do.

His door was ajar in case the kids woke up so Emmy knocked on the open door and poked her head inside.

"Diego, did you make those footsteps?"

"Yeah, if the kids woke I wanted them to know where to find us. Come in Emmy."

She stepped in and left the door cracked open. Diego motioned to the sofa at a 45-degree angle from them, "You want a drink?"

"No, I'm beat, so I'm about to head down to my apartment but just got some news and wanted you to know right away."

She leaned toward Shelby, a frown on her face and sadness in her pretty brown eyes. "Shelby, I'm sorry to tell you that we've found Stacy. It appears she was murdered. Van and Charly are working with the police to gather the evidence and see what they can find out, but suffice it to say, there will be an investigation. I wish I had better news for you."

He watched Shelby's reaction; she swallowed repeatedly and tears fell from her eyes. Her hand, still in Diego's, gripped his tightly as she tried not to break down. He squeezed her hand back, his heart silently aching for her and the kids. Her bottom lip quivered and he knew she was losing her battle to not break down.

He knelt in front of her. Shelby's arms wrapped around him and she buried her face into his neck as a heart-wrenching wail tore through her throat. Pulling her to him, he sat back on the love seat, cradling her on his lap while she cried. He held tightly and rubbed her back as she sobbed. His eyes sought Emmy's; tears rolled down her cheeks as she witnessed this brave woman finally crack under the pressure and sadness. That was the thing about Emmy, she was tough, tougher than most, but she had a soft spot too. Her heart.

Swiping her cheeks, she stood quietly. "I'll leave you two alone. I'm available to chat whenever you're ready. Good night."

He sat with a broken Shelby as his tears rolled down his cheeks and into her hair. He held her for a long time, until she'd cried herself out and quietly clung to him. He was sorry for her heartbreak, but happy to hold her as she pulled her thoughts together. This was a pivotal moment in Shelby's life, in the kids' lives. There'd be more bad news to come, more to shield them from. More than just that their dad was a jackass; he'd killed their mother. But, if there could be any good news from this at all, it was that now there would be a murder investigation and that Kurtis would be put under the microscope, because the first person ever considered a person of interest is the spouse, especially when the marriage is in a state of falling apart.

When Shelby had calmed, she lifted herself away from him, and swiped at her eyes.

"Sorry I got your shirt wet."

Shaking his head he smiled, "Don't worry, I'm not."

There was still moisture on his lashes and her forefinger crooked slightly as she dabbed at it with the back of her finger. Staring into her eyes, something changed in his heart, as if a bolt of lightning struck and lit his path and made it completely clear to him. He wanted to be with Shelby and the kids. He wanted them in his life. How is it something so profound can hit you that quickly? He'd give Josh a call in the morning and have a chat; if anyone knew that, Josh would.

"Emmy said she'd be around if you have questions. She wanted to allow you time to adjust. I say we let her rest and get some rest ourselves. We'll speak with her in the morning. We'll get more specifics then and by that time, Van and Charly will be able to fill us in on what they've found and where the investigation stands."

She nodded and stood. Wiping her hands on her jeans she started toward the door.

"Shelby?"

She turned and looked at him; yeah, she was perfect for him. Both of them broken. Maybe two broken pieces could become one good piece.

"Why don't you stay in here? You can have the bedroom so you can sleep in a bed and I'll sleep on the sofa. It's all good, the kids can find us and you'll be able to get some rest. You'll likely have a lot of questions to answer tomorrow."

She hesitated. "Diego, I..."

"You can. Please."

He closed the gap between them; his right hand wrapped itself around her nape as he pulled her close. He studied her, his eyes taking in her expression, her sadness and if he could have absorbed Shelby's pain in that moment, he would have. He dipped his head down and touched his lips to hers. So soft and reverent, just a touch. Then he pulled back.

Shelby's arms wrapped tightly around him and pulled his body to hers. He engulfed her in his arms. Her body felt amazing against his, like she was meant for him. Two halves of a whole, and when they stood together like this, he felt invincible, strong in a way he hadn't felt in years.

_____

43

Shelby woke to giggling and the sound of some video game playing on a television somewhere. As she opened her eyes, she realized she was in Diego's plain room and all the memories of last night flooded her and threatened to drown her in sorrow once again.

She let some of the tears fall so they wouldn't fall later; she needed to be strong for the kids and she needed to listen as Emmy told her some of the details of Stacy's murder. Kurtis had to pay for this, there was no doubt in her mind. He had to and then she had to get custody of the kids. That was going to be the hardest part because by now she'd been fired from her job at the daycare. She hadn't bothered calling in because she didn't want to be traced and if Kurtis asked them, she didn't want them to have to lie for her, so she was a no call, no show, which was shitty, but she'd had to do it that way.

So, she didn't have a job and no way to support Callie and Anders. But, if Kurtis was guilty, likely Stacy's portion of the marital funds would go to the kids and hopefully she could sell that big ole house they lived in and buy something smaller in the country where she could raise them and give them a happy life. Somehow that seemed like a great plan. She sighed as she contemplated the plethora of thoughts that vied for her attention.

Pulling the covers back she stood and realized that she was in her sweatpants and a t-shirt, so she'd gone back to her room to get her pajamas before coming back here. She didn't even remember that. Exhaustion had been heavy.

Once in the living room, she saw Diego on the floor with Callie, Anders and Ted. The kids played video games, trying to explain to Diego what they were doing in between exclamations of a great job and disappointment when they lost a game.

"Good morning. What's going on?"

Diego looked up at her and smiled. "Piper brought some games for them to play."

Callie pointed out the door. "Piper lives over there."

Diego filled in the vague direction.

"Piper, Donovan, Creed and myself live up here on the second floor. Emmy, Charly, Deacon, Caiden and Falcon have apartments downstairs. I think I forgot to fill you in on this yesterday. There's a fair amount to know about being here. But, anyway, Piper brought the kids some games to play and as you can see, they're thrilled."

She smiled as she sat on the sofa watching them. They were so innocent and happy. She struggled with when the right time to tell them was or would be.

Anders looked at Diego. "I'm hungry."

Diego looked at his watch and nodded. "I think if we all get dressed, we can go down and have breakfast. Sheldon usually has breakfast ready around seven-ish. Team members come and go for breakfast, so he has something prepared and ready for when we get up."

Anders stood up and Shelby did as well. "Come on buddy, I'll help you get ready. Callie, are you coming too?"

Callie set her game controller on the television stand and followed her out the door. Shelby glanced back at Diego and he winked at her. That sent a riot of emotions through her body and a flush from her belly rolled all the way up her body, heating her from the inside out. Wow.

Once in their room she opened the drawers holding their clothing and pulled clothes out.

Callie stood alongside the dresser, "I want to pick my own."

"Okay."

Shelby stood back and watched as she chose a pair of jeans and a dark green t-shirt and red socks. She opened her mouth to say something, then decided it really didn't matter. She'd let Callie have her own choice in clothing and not worry about the small stuff; there were worse things to deal with today than clothing colors.

Once the kids were dressed she pulled out her own clothing. "Why don't you go over by Diego while I get dressed and I'll be ready in a bit."

Anders took off running out the door and Callie chased after him. That wasn't hard at all.

Looking in the mirror, she noticed her eyes were puffy, likely from crying, and slightly red-rimmed, also from crying. She dragged a brush through her hair and tried making it look decent, which wasn't too difficult, though as soon as she could she'd see if a stylist could fix it up a bit.

She donned a pair of jeans and a gray t-shirt and stepped into the bedroom only to find the kids' clothing laying around on the floor. She picked up their clothes, folded them neatly and lay them on the top of the dresser so the kids could wear the same pajamas again tonight. They were running out of clean clothes; she'd have to ask someone where she could do their laundry today.

Diego and the kids walked out of his door at the same time she left their apartment.

He smiled at her and her body burned up once more. "The kids were hungry so I thought I'd take them down. If you're ready, we can all go together."

"Yep, all set."

She smiled at him and his cheeks reddened a bit too. She liked that feeling. It made the butterflies in her tummy take flight.

From the elevator she could smell the delicious aromas of breakfast foods filtering through the ventilation system.

As the elevator stopped on the first floor, the kids jumped out of the door, then Anders stopped and looked up at her. "Sorry, I forgot."

She chuckled. "That's okay, honey, next time."

He nodded then and ran to the dining room with Callie. Diego laughed and took her hand as they walked and the electricity that zinged around her body felt like she could conquer the world. She liked the way he felt next to her.

44

As they finished breakfast and carried their plates to the kitchen Emmy walked in.

"Good morning. Shelby and Diego, when you have a moment, we can chat about things." Emmy smiled but glanced down at the kids. She likely didn't want them knowing anything was wrong. "I heard today that Dodge and Jax were bringing the twins over to GHOST, so maybe Callie and Anders would like to meet them."

Diego laughed, "They'll love Jax. What do you say kids, want to meet Maya and Myles?"

"Yeah." Anders cheered.

Callie nodded and he felt better knowing they'd have some playtime today. Then he and Shelby could talk about when and what to tell the kids. That was, if she wanted him involved.

"Okay, follow me."

The back door opened and in walked Josh and Isabella. Diego grinned, "Good morning, what brings you two over here?"

Diego shook Josh's hand and hugged Isabella. Josh responded, "Isi wanted to come and meet Shelby and the kids and wondered if she could be of assistance with them?"

Diego turned to Shelby. "Shelby, this is Josh and Isabella Masters. Josh is a special operative with GHOST and Isi is our resident physician here and has her own practice in town." He introduced the kids. "And this is Callie and Anders Kennedy." Crouching down, he added, "Doctor Isi is a good doctor and very nice. Josh is my best friend."

Both kids looked at Josh and Isabella and stared. Isi knelt down, "Good morning. If you have a need for me, I'm only a phone call away. Diego knows how to get in touch with me and so does everyone else here. Okay?"

Both kids nodded but it was Diego who broke the silence. "I understand Jax and Dodge are bringing Maya and Myles next door this morning."

Isi laughed. "Yes, we came over here to see if we could walk with the kids over to the house; the Sagers are on their way."

"We were just walking them over." Shelby responded.

Josh looked at Diego, nodded slightly and quietly said, "We should take them so you can speak with Emmy."

Diego glanced at Shelby and her composure begin to crumble, so he said to the kids, "Hey you two, would you like to walk over with Josh and Isi while your Aunt Shelby and I talk to Emmy for a minute? Then we'll come over and get you."

Callie looked up at Shelby, then at him. "Okay."

She then took Anders' hand and began walking to the door. Shelby took Isi's hand in her hands and squeezed. "Thank you so much."

Isi then hugged Shelby. "I'm so sorry for your loss. We'll take care of them. I promise."

Isi hugged Diego, Josh shook his hand and they followed the kids out the door. He turned to Shelby but before he could say anything she said, "News gets around here fast."

"It's likely Emmy sent a group text out last night so everyone knew and would know not to say anything in front of the kids until you tell them."

"Okay." She inhaled a deep breath and let it out slowly. "I guess we better go see what Emmy has to say."

Her hand rested on her tummy and he could see she was battling to keep her head on straight.

"I'm right here with you. The whole time, I'm right here."

Her eyes locked on his and tears gathered in hers. "I'm so grateful to have you with me, Diego. Thank you."

He pulled her in for a hug and held her close. She smelled like freshly dried linens out on the line. His mom used to dry their bedding outside when he was little. Oh how he loved the fresh fragrance as he climbed in bed at night after the sheets had been changed. Then, his mom would tuck him in tightly and he felt like he was in a fresh clean cocoon as he drifted off to sleep. Too bad his mom wasn't here, she'd like Shelby. She had hutzpah, as Mom would say. She'd done the right thing knowing it could put her in jail, but she did it for the kids. It was purely an unselfish act of love.

Shelby inhaled and he stepped away. Gently taking her hand, he walked them forward toward the elevator. A quick wave of his watch in front of the panel and the doors slid open.

Waiting for Shelby to step in first, he quietly followed her and pushed the button for the conference room floor. Their hands were locked together the entire ride down but no words were said. What could he say?

The doors slid open again and he pulled her hand forward, urging her to step off. She finally looked up at him and he could see the sadness and hurt. Her jaw tightened.

"I'm right here with you Shel. I'm not going anywhere."

Biting her bottom lip her eyes glistened as she blinked rapidly. Man she was strong.

He led her to the conference room, opened the door and let her enter first. The only people in the room right now were Emmy and Piper. It wasn't often that this room, the hub of their operations, was this quiet. Emmy stood from her tan metal desk at the far end of the room and walked toward them. Her limp was pronounced this morning but to her credit, she continued working each day as if she had no pain at all.

"Good morning again. I asked to have the room this morning so you'd have some privacy Shelby. Piper is here because she's the computer rock star and while I could muddle through to show what I can, Piper can do it with her eyes closed."

Piper turned in her chair but stayed in front of her computer. She smiled at Shelby and Diego nodded to her. Holding a chair out for Shelby, he waited for her to sit, then took the seat next to her as Emmy sat across from them.

"I'm sorry again for your loss Shelby and I wrestled with telling you last night or waiting till this morning. But, you had a right to know and I didn't want to keep it from you. I did let everyone here and next door know so no one will say anything to the kids or in front of them accidentally. And, you are all safe here."

Shelby's voice broke but she did manage to say, "Thank you."

Piper quietly set a box of tissues on the table and Shelby reached over for one. She wadded it in her hand then opened it up; it seemed like more of a safety blanket than a need at this point.

Emmy cleared her throat. "So, Stacy was found about ten miles from where we found her suitcase. A hiker found her in the woods, partially covered with branches and leaves. She wasn't raped, but she was beaten. Based on what Callie has said, some of the trauma could have happened when she fell down the stairs. The medical examiner will need to determine whether the fall was the cause of her death or a subsequent head injury."

Shelby sat still as stone, staring at the table. When it appeared she wasn't able to say anything he stepped in. "Emmy, has Kurtis been called?"

"Yes. The hiker called police and once police determined who it was, they called Kurtis. He was brought into the coroner's office to identify her body. Charly and Van were watching him closely to see how he behaved. He's a stone."

Shelby lifted her eyes to Emmy. "What happens now?"

The phone rang but she ignored it. "Police have spent the night gathering evidence. Charly and Van have asked to stay close to watch the investigation and Kurtis. They are keeping their distance and he doesn't know they belong to RAPTOR. But, I understand at this point he was brought in for questioning."

She turned to Piper, who brought up a video of a police officer walking into the precinct with Kurtis Kennedy. He was not handcuffed, he wasn't under arrest and he seemed to be going in willingly.

Emmy spoke while they watched the video. "Not five minutes after Kurtis walked into the station, his attorney showed up. So, I'm not sure how much information, if any, they've gotten from him since he obviously lawyered up. He also must have called his attorney before he came to the station. Right now, we need to hope the coroner can find evidence that Kurtis had something to do with her death or evidence around the area pinning him to the scene. Piper and Caiden are researching all the cameras around the area where she was found to see if they can spot Kurtis' car anywhere in the vicinity."

Shelby finally asked, "Does anyone know the kids and I are here? You won't give them back will you? Please tell me you won't give them back to him."

Emmy sat forward. "Shelby, look at me." Shelby raised her eyes to Emmy's and she continued. "What you've done is brave. I did something similar before I started RAPTOR. Diego was there with me and so were Van, Charly and Creed. We broke the rules to save three children. I believe with my whole heart that you did what you did to save the kids, not harm them. I also believe Kurtis Kennedy is a liar and is hiding something. My team and I are committed to finding out what that is and helping you and the kids. You have my promise."

Diego leaned toward Shelby. "You have my promise too."

45

———

I t had been twenty-four hours since she'd learned of Stacy's death. She still didn't have the courage to tell the kids. They'd had so much fun today playing at the GHOST compound with Maya and Miles, Jax and Dodge's fourteen-month-old twins and Aidyn, Axel and Bridget's six-year-old son. They all ran and played and it was so nice to watch them carefree that she didn't have the heart to tell them.

They now lay peacefully asleep in their room at the compound and she felt a bit of guilt that she hadn't told them this news that would change their lives.

The door silently swung open and Diego stepped inside. The smile on his face as he looked at the kids sleeping was a sight to behold for sure. She loved watching him look at the kids. He seemed at peace when he looked at them.

His eyes swung to hers and his smile broadened.

Careful not to wake the kids, she stood from her perch at the edge of the bed and walked toward him. He'd been her rock today. He'd been her rock almost from the start of all this craziness and she didn't know what she'd done to deserve him in her life.

He tilted his head to the door and stepped out; she willingly followed him, the footprints still on the floor for the kids.

"We're needed downstairs."

"Okay. Is there some news?" She hesitated as she looked at the door to her room.

Diego pointed to Piper's door, which now stood open. "Piper will listen for the kids while we're downstairs."

Nodding, she swallowed and willed herself to be strong. To be brave, like Emmy said she was. As the time ran on though, she didn't feel all that brave.

Waving his watch in front of the panel to the elevator the doors slid open and she stepped in. As soon as the doors closed she turned to Diego and stared into his beautiful eyes. So soulful and sinful at the same time. His lips curved up in a smile as their eyes locked on each other and she lifted herself up on her toes and touched her lips to his.

They were soft and warm and inviting. Her lips tingled after that brief kiss and her cheeks felt like they were on fire. His hand slid into the hair at her nape and his fingers caressed her scalp as he pulled her close and kissed her again. Less brief, more passion. Her hands grabbed hold of his shirt at either side of his waist and held on.

The elevator slowed and he pulled back slightly, looked into her eyes and winked.

"I've wanted to do that for a while. Thank you for breaking the ice."

"Thank you for being here for me." As the doors opened she added, "And for kissing me back."

He chuckled. Her tummy somersaulted and she wasn't sure if it was because of the summons to come down to the control room or Diego. Likely Diego; she was growing numb to bad news these days.

He opened the door and held it as she entered the room. Emmy was speaking with Charly and Van on a chat screen and when they entered Emmy waved them over to the table. "They're here now."

As they sat at the table, Emmy angled the camera so they were all on the screen and they said their hellos.

Emmy began the conversation. "So, it appears that Stacy had an attorney. It also appears that Kurtis wasn't aware of this attorney. Van and Charly were at the police station today to see what information they could gather and Stacy's attorney walked in." She looked over a notebook in front of her. "Attorney Spencer Wingert."

Emmy looked at the screen and Van took over. "Wingert came to the police station because he'd been trying to call Shelby's phone but she didn't answer. Stacy gave him your number, Shelby. He has an envelope for you and only you. Stacy instructed him to open the envelope in your presence only. Since we all agree it isn't safe for you to come here, we're at his office and he'll open it on the screen if you are in agreement. He says the information in the envelope is something you need."

Her heart raced and she swallowed to moisten her dry throat. She felt like she was standing in a tunnel and their voices echoed.

Emmy walked to a small refrigerator and pulled out a bottle of water. She held it up to Diego but he shook his head no. She set the water in front of Shelby.

Diego opened the water and handed it to her. She took a generous drink, then responded to Van. "Okay, I'm ready."

Van turned the camera around and Stacy's attorney sat at a big wooden desk littered with files and papers. A small area in front of him was cleared and in that opening sat a manila envelope. He looked into Shelby's eyes through the camera. His white mustache softened the angles of his face. His light blue eyes, crinkled at the corners from his years in the law office and life, seemed kind, and she could tell he was distressed at the news he was about to share.

"Ms. Davidson, I am sorry for your loss. My name is Spencer Wingert and your beautiful sister, Stacy, was my client for the past couple of years. Suffice it to say she's shared a fair amount of information with me, some of which you are aware, such as the state of her marriage. But, in this envelope is the information she only wanted shared with you in case something happened to her. She was a brave young woman and while she worried that her husband might get violent or cause her harm if he suspected all she knew about him, I don't think she ever thought it would be her death. At least that's what she said, but clearly the cloak and dagger things she was doing had her believing it could come to that."

Shelby sat stone still as she looked into the camera at this kindly man whose voice shook slightly as he spoke about her sister. "Thank you." was all she could say at this point.

He nodded and, with shaking fingers, opened the envelope. "I was instructed to find you if something happened to her. It was with sorrow that I learned this morning, via the morning news, of her passing. I spent the day calling your phone and it was only by a fortunate coincidence that I ran into Donovan and Charlesia at the police station today. God has a way of putting people in place when we need them."

She glanced at Diego and smiled. "Yes, he certainly does."

Diego put his hand over hers and squeezed. She turned her hand and locked fingers with him and Attorney Wingert nodded and smiled.

Clearing his throat he continued. "Your sister was gathering evidence against her husband, Kurtis. She suspected that he was doing something illegal to grow his business so quickly, because in her words, "That jackass isn't likable enough to have folks wanting to do business with him, and yet, look at him."

Dumping the papers out of the manila envelope, he sorted through them to find the documents he wanted to explain, organizing them in a meaningful order to him.

Holding up the first stack of paper, he looked at Shelby and said, "Stacy found evidence that Kurtis was bribing politicians for business. In a couple of cases, he even set up a party and hired underage girls to come to the party, ply the politicians with booze and have sex with them while he recorded it all on hidden cameras. Then he contacted the politicians and showed them the evidence he had. He exchanged lucrative business contracts for his silence. When they balked, and a couple of them did, he set up an alternate blackmail scheme in which he had, in one case, one politician's daughter, aged sixteen, performing in an adult video. Threatening to expose the daughter and harm her reputation for the rest of her life, the politician complied handsomely. That's why she didn't want to leave him yet, she wanted all the evidence she could get so he'd go to jail for a very long time and she and the kids would be free of him. She worried he'd wriggle out of jail time in some way, so she wanted enough evidence to make charges stick."

Shelby sat back in her chair, stunned at what Stacy was doing and also so damned proud of her. "Why didn't she want me to know this? I could have helped her."

"She didn't want you to help her or to know because if Kurtis found out, she wanted you safe."

He held up a second stack of papers. "These are papers naming you as the children's guardian should something happen to her and when Kurtis goes to jail. She told me there was no one on the entire earth who would treat her children as their own other than you and she knew you'd be a fantastic mother to them."

A sob tore through Shelby's throat and tears spilled down her cheeks. Diego leaned over and pulled her to him for a hug and she cried in his shoulder for a few moments before she could gain her composure.

When she pulled away, Diego handed her another tissue and she dabbed at her cheeks and swiped the tissue under her nose. Swallowing again, she looked into the camera at the attorney and waited for him to continue.

"This third stack of papers holds the children's trusts, birth certificates, medical and dental records and bank account information with adequate funds for you to care for them until the home can be sold and the expected trial of Kurtis Kennedy, not only for the blackmail, but likely her death, is over and all assets revert to the children." He leaned forward and stared directly at her. "Your sister was a brave, kind, loving woman and she loved those children and you with her whole heart. Again, I am deeply sorry for your loss Ms. Davidson."

Her lips trembled but she managed to take a few deep breaths before answering him. "Thank you Attorney Wingert. You've described Stacy perfectly and I thank you so much for being the keeper of her secrets."

He nodded and Van turned the camera around. "Charly and I will escort Attorney Wingert to the police station with the evidence against Kurtis and we'll bring the children's documents back with us."

She looked at Van, for the first time, really looked at him. He had beautiful light green eyes and his arms were covered with tattoos of various designs; likely each one had a meaning to him and told the story of his life. And he had a nice sincere smile.

"Thank you Van and thank you to Charly, too. We are so appreciative of your help."

He smiled and nodded. "You're welcome. Try and get some rest tonight, things are going to be all right in a little while."

46

Shelby looked directly at Emmy after the phone conference ended. Emmy asked, "Do you have any questions Shelby? I know this is a lot to take in, but if you have any, we'll try to answer them."

Shelby swallowed. Diego's hand was still clasped with hers and she made no move to let it go. "I think I just need some time to process all of this. It almost seems too good to be true."

Diego squeezed her hand. "It isn't over yet, and Kurtis will likely toss out all sorts of accusations. And, there is a likely kidnapping charge against you. If not, he'll probably try to make one, mostly to make it seem as though he is the victim. But, with the evidence against him, it should die a quick death. And with Stacy's desire to have you as the children's guardian, plus the fact that you've taken great care of the children, and someone, also likely Kurtis, tried having you and the children killed, it's not very promising for Kurtis, but it'll take some time to get through."

She nodded and smiled at him. Shelby then turned her head to Emmy. "So, now we wait and see what happens after Attorney Wingert turns in the evidence Stacy collected?"

Emmy nodded. "Yes. But, we'll know soon enough with Van and Charly there. Plus, they know that someone at the local police station was working dirty and helping to keep Stacy's disappearance low on the list or had wrapped it up as her just taking off. But we've sent our information that the fake credit card uses from Stacy's cards actually generated from SmartTech, so they'll have a bit more evidence that Kurtis had something to do with Stacy's disappearance. Ideally, we'd like to find some camera footage of Kurtis disposing of Stacy's body or in the vicinity where her body was found. We're still working on that."

Shelby inhaled a deep breath and slowly let it out. "Okay. Well I'm both exhausted and hopeful and not sure sleep will come all that easy for me with all of this information roiling around in my mind. Thank you." She looked up at him and their eyes locked. "Thank you too, Diego, for all you've done for all of us. I'm forever grateful you were investigating me, because it brought us together."

He smiled at her, and his heart did a somersault in his chest. He'd never had that feeling before and it both surprised him and delighted him.

"It goes without saying that I'm happy I was available in the room when Emmy needed someone to go on a mission." He smiled broadly and she smiled in return. He couldn't help it, he leaned in and kissed her. It was brief, but in some way, he felt like Emmy already knew there was something more than a fleeting connection between him and Shelby, and this made it official without him making an announcement.

Taking Shelby's hand in his they left the room and walked to the elevator to make their way upstairs. Once they'd stepped inside and the doors closed he asked, "Do you feel like having a drink to celebrate?"

"Yes. I have some nervous energy to work off before I'm actually able to lay down and sleep."

A silence hung between them for a time and just before the doors opened he whispered, "I know how to work off that energy."

She giggled and squeezed his hand. "Looking forward to it."

Entering his apartment, he glanced over to Piper's door and saw that it was still open. She was still listening for the kids and he was happy to take advantage of that. He closed his door, clicked the lock and turned to face Shelby, who stood very close to him.

Her hands slid up his chest and cupped his jaw on both sides, her thumbs smoothed over his cheeks as her eyes bored into his. A soft smile lifted the corners of her lips and she stepped closer, so they were pressed against each other.

His hands wrapped around her and pulled her close. She stood only to his chin, but it didn't matter, they still fit. He spread his feet apart so she scooted closer to him and there were very few places their bodies didn't meet. Still not good enough.

Bending at his knees, he picked her up and pulled her tightly to him. As her arms wrapped around his shoulders, her head bent and her giggles tickled his ear. She wrapped her legs around his waist and his body went from fifteen to five hundred in seconds.

He carried her into his bedroom, sat on the end of his bed, then lay back still holding Shelby. The instant her body weight lay on him, he imprinted how she felt in that moment, because he never wanted to forget it. His body heated, his pants grew tight and her voluptuous breasts pressed against his chest in the most delicious way. His hands caressed her back, then slid down to her ass and pulled her tightly against him.

Shelby moaned in his ear and he wanted to hear her do that over and over again. Repeating his movements, he ground against her as his cock thickened to an unbearable degree. She lifted back and pulled her shirt over her head as she continued to straddle him, then her fingers began tugging his t-shirt from his waistband and up his body, helping him to pull it free from his body. She tossed it to the floor and quickly reached back and unsnapped her bra. Her breasts fell forward when her bra came off and his fingers wrapped around them and enjoyed the way her warm smooth skin felt as he molded and pressed her breasts in his hands.

He pulled her down to him, his mouth seeking one of her generous breasts. She moaned again as she held herself up just enough that he could lick and taste and move from one breast to the other. The feel of her taut nipples as he sucked them in reminded him of fresh raspberries in the summer and he nibbled and laved at them eagerly.

She sat back and his eyes feasted on her breasts, still glistening from his attention and damned if his cock didn't throb at the sight.

"Gotta get these pants off Shel."

She grinned and moved off him. He quickly unsnapped and unzipped his pants and hooked his thumbs into his waistband as he stood and shoved them down his legs. When he turned to look at her, he was pleased to see she'd done the same thing.

His mouth captured hers in a heated kiss. He tasted her, his tongue explored her, he tried memorizing every detail about her.

Shelby pushed him back on the bed and he quickly pushed himself up the bed. She quickly straddled his legs, and her hands first sought his cock as she wrapped a hand around it and slowly slid up and down a few times, watching til the precum appeared on the head. She smiled then and swiped her thumb over it once, then rose up and positioned him at her entrance.

She held his gaze as she slowly slid her body down on his cock. He never looked away from her and it was honestly the sexiest thing he'd ever experienced in his life. Once she'd slid down she stayed right there for a moment as her hands slid up his chest.

Huskily she asked, "Fast or slow?"

"Slow. I want to watch you fuck me."

A sexy smile appeared on her beautiful face as her hands roamed his chest. She sat up straight and slowly rose and fell on his cock; her warmth encased him like a glove massaging and caressing him in the most erotic way. He watched her breasts move as she rose and fell on him, her narrow waist swelled into her hips as her legs splayed to make room for him.

His hands enjoyed her body, her skin was as soft as the finest silk, her warmth like the coziest blanket. He moved his hips up and down with her and he enjoyed the way her lips formed an "o" when he slid in further. He smiled as he watched her, she was exciting, enticing and so fucking sexy.

Finally deciding to speed things up, he circled her waist with his hands and began helping her movements, jogging her up and down faster. Her luscious lips once again formed that beautiful "o" and he realized that was one of his favorite parts.

Her skin began to glow as it heated, her cheeks deepened in color and those green eyes bored into his as she watched him while they gave each other pleasure.

"Let's do this girl. Come on." He urged her and she did not disappoint.

Her speed increased as she dropped down on him, her breathing came in spurts and those lips. Damn.

Her eyes closed slightly as her orgasm began rolling over her. It was beautiful. She cried out her orgasm and he watched everything happen as if for the first time in his life. He'd never felt like this before and at his age, it was a wonder it had taken this long.

She fell limp against him and he had mercy on her and wrapped his left arm around her as he rolled them over.

Once he was on top, her eyes opened to stare deeply into his, her lips curved into a smile. Her hands wrapped around his shoulders and she raised her legs to circle around his ass cheeks.

He pumped into her over and over. His balls tightened painfully as his orgasm raged. Diego groaned as he emptied himself into her, then his body released its tight hold on his muscles and he fell over her, trying to hold himself up on his elbows. His lips lay close to her ear as he tried to catch his breath.

"Fuck," he whispered.

Shelby giggled. "Yeah."

His breathing caught up to him and his mind, which should have been engaged, finally cleared.

"Fuck."

She giggled.

"I mean, we didn't use a condom."

"I can't have children. And, I'm clean." She relaxed under him and he moved to roll to the side. Her arms held him close. "Are you?"

"I'm clean, but my mind is anything but where you're concerned."

47

S he woke when she felt the bed dip and Diego left to use the bathroom. She lay there thinking for some time how wonderful it was with him. How she'd felt last night. So sexy and desirable, she tried remembering the last time she'd felt like that. It had been years, if she'd ever felt like that at all. Her body felt deliciously tired this morning but her heart felt splendidly full.

The shower turned on and she looked at the clock on the dresser; it was four a.m. He was showering already?

Pulling his pillow over, she inhaled his scent and hugged his pillow to her chest. She remembered how it felt to be in his arms last night. How it felt to be wrapped in comfort and protection and as if she didn't have any worries in the world.

The shower turned off and she listened as the soft sounds of Diego getting ready filtered back to her ears. Then the door opened and the fresh aroma of his shower soap floated over her and wrapped her in a different cocoon of all things good, masculine and sexy.

She smiled up at him as he sat alongside the bed. "You're up early."

"I worried the kids might be looking for us or need us and I didn't know if you wanted them to see us...together."

She swallowed and her hand reached for his. "I want to shout to the world that we're together. I guess if that's what you think we are. It's hardly been a conventional courtship."

He chuckled. "You can say that again."

He leaned down and kissed her lips. "I'll take your lead Shelby. But, for the record..." He looked into her eyes, his left forefinger smoothed across her cheek then he tucked his hand around her nape. He slowly leaned down and kissed her lips. "I want us to see where this goes. I want to be with you as you bring Kurtis down and get custody of the kids and as your name is cleared and then later when you settle with the kids somewhere, I hope to be in that picture."

Tears sprang instantly to her eyes as she watched his soft brown eyes take her all in. They roved over her face, her lips and met her eyes once again.

"I want you to be in that picture too."

She sat up and pushed herself back against the headboard of the bed, then looked into his eyes. "I don't know how to tell the kids about...Stacy." Clearing her throat she continued. "I won't say anything about Kurtis until it's all decided, the evidence is all in and we know with certainty that he's guilty. When they're older, I'll share the rest with them, but for now, I'll only tell them that they don't have to worry about going to see their father ever again."

"I think that's best. I really do." He smiled at her and took her hand in his.

"But, I think for us, it can be as simple as them seeing us holding hands. A sweet kiss here and there. A hug. Small things. If they ask, I'll say something but it can just be natural and they'll just 'know' that we're together."

He smiled again and she wanted to see that on his face always. "I think you're a natural with them and that sounds like the perfect way to not bombard them with more than they can process."

He leaned in and kissed her briefly. "Since I'm up, how about I go down to the kitchen and get us some coffee?"

"Thank you. I'll hop in the shower."

She watched him walk from the room. He was fine.

She pulled the covers back, and picked up her clothing as she walked to the bathroom. Turning the shower on to warm, then stepped in the shower enjoying the feel of the warm water. Today felt so much different than yesterday. Today *was* so much different than yesterday. She could finally look forward and know, for one thing, that she didn't have to hide forever. Now she just had to hope and pray that Kurtis was unable to circumvent the law and get away with murder.

She smiled as the fragrance of Diego's soap filled the humid air around her.

Finishing up her shower, she toweled herself off and dressed in her clothes from yesterday. Once the kids woke, she'd change clothes for the day.

She finger combed her hair then stepped from the bathroom to the aroma of fresh coffee.

"Hmm, that smells so good."

Diego chuckled as he handed her a steaming cup of the fresh brew. "I brought us a couple of cookies too. I thought we could sit in the living room until the kids wake. Unless you feel more comfortable going in their room and pretending you slept there last night."

His look was almost hopeful and she wondered if he wanted her to go to her room. She tilted her head to the side, "Do you want me to go back?"

He chuckled again and stepped up to her. "No, I hoped you'd stay here so we can begin showing the kids we're together."

Giggling she nodded, "Good answer. Let's go sit in the living room and enjoy a few moments of quiet before the video games and questions begin."

He held his hand out to her to precede him and she felt light and happy and so damned hopeful.

As he sat in the love seat recliner next to her, he said, "I thought, since you mentioned that our relationship was far from conventional, that maybe we could go out to eat tonight. Someone here, or next door, will help with the kids. I could ask Josh and Isi to take them if you don't mind, and we can have an official date."

"Oh, that would be so nice. I have to warn you though, I don't have any fancy clothes so we need to keep it simple. Maybe hamburgers and fries."

"That's a deal. We have a nice little bar in town, the Copper Cup, and they have the best food and bar-b-que. Plus, it's very casual."

She laughed. "Deal."

48

D iego walked from his room to the room next door where Shelby and the kids were staying. Sort of. The day had been filled with video games, playing in the workout room with the kids, taking a walk around the grounds and over to the GHOST compound and basically passing the time. He was still considered on a mission, so there wasn't anything new for him, and Van and Charly hadn't returned yet from ensuring Kurtis was arrested. He hated bugging them, even though he'd thought about it what felt like a million times today, he put his faith and trust in God and hoped it would all work out. Van and Charly did confirm that Attorney Wingert did get to the police department and did speak with a detective. Piper was manning the computers heavily with another Cyber team member, Caiden Marx. They were individually working on who had connections with Kurtis Kennedy at the police department and why Stacy's disappearance had been pushed so far under the rug. And looking at video footage obtained from the area surrounding where Stacy's body had been found to see if Kurtis was in the area around the time Stacy's body had been dumped. According to the coroner's report, she'd been dropped close to four weeks ago, so the same time she disappeared. The waiting was excruciating.

Shelby had opted not to say anything to the kids today. Although she'd expressed more than once today that she knew she needed to say something soon, she wanted all the information before saying anything. For the most part, the kids still hadn't asked about their father or going home and they seemed quite content to stay here and play and have fun. They were missing school too and that was a situation they'd need to deal with. Bridget had mentioned that the kids were more than welcome to join six-year-old Aidyn since she homeschooled him. Shelby liked that idea but she didn't want to start them at it and then have to pull them out right away. So many things to consider.

Their apartment smelled of fresh shower soap and the air was humid, signaling showers had been taken. Anders sat on the sofa watching a cartoon movie and when he saw Diego, his little face lit right up.

"Hi Anders, what'cha watching?"

"*Brave.*"

"Oh, I like that one."

He sat next to Anders, who immediately climbed up in his lap, but he never looked away from the movie. It was his favorite part where the momma turned into a bear.

Content to sit here quietly and watch the movie with Anders, Diego relaxed into the sofa with him and watched in silence as he enjoyed this sweet-smelling little boy with all the innocence of a child, but whose world was going to change so much more than it already had. He couldn't do anything to bring Stacy back, but Shelby would certainly do everything in her power to give them a good life and without Kurtis' abuse in the mix, these kids would have the best chance they could have at a good life.

The bathroom door opened and Callie walked out in her pajamas, which were yellow with little moons on them, and Shelby walked out looking fresh and clean with a nice fitting pair of jeans and a soft white sweater. She looked huggable and kissable and he liked that he felt that way.

Shelby's smile was huge when her eyes landed on him sitting with Anders. "Hey there, what are you guys watching?"

"*Brave*." He chuckled.

Her smile grew and her eyes followed Callie as she walked to the sofa and sat as close to Diego as she could. He lifted his arm so she tucked in under it and he felt more content than he ever had before. Ted lumbered in and flopped on the floor in front of the sofa; the kids had worn him out today too and he almost hated the fact that they were going out tonight. Maybe tomorrow night they could plan to order food in and make it a movie night.

Shelby walked to the sofa and sat on the other side of Callie, but twisted slightly to look his way.

"We could stay in tonight and go out tomorrow night."

He smiled at her. "You reading my mind now?"

Giggling she nodded, "Kind of easy to see you're perfectly content right where you are. Since we didn't eat, we can order something in."

Diego looked down at the kids, "You guys hungry?"

Anders never looked away from the television. "I want pizza."

Nodding Diego looked at Callie, who looked up at him and sweetly asked, "What do you want?"

He laughed then. "I'd like chicken wings."

"Oh, I want those too!"

Shelby laughed then too. "We can get both. My treat this time."

She went to her burner phone, which lay on the coffee table and tapped an icon on the face of it. "What did you say the name of that restaurant is in town? The Copper Kettle or something?"

"The Copper Cup."

Nodding she typed it into her phone and he chuckled knowing she was going to need more information, but she seemed excited to do this for them so he'd wait.

"Hello, I'd like to place an order to be delivered please."

The person who answered asked a question, and she responded, "Ah, cheese and ..."

Looking to him for an answer he laughed. "I like pepperoni and mushrooms and black olives."

She ordered a half cheese and half pepperoni, mush-rooms and black olives pizza then hesitated. Pulling her phone away she put it on speaker.

"Anything else?"

"Yes, we'd also like two orders of chicken wings."

"Sounds good, what flavor would you like?"

Her eyes rounded as she looked at him and he laughed. "I like the garlic parmesan wings, but they have any flavor you'd like."

"Order two orders of those please and one plain."

"Sounds good ma'am, is that it?"

Shelby's cheeks turned pink and she looked his way. "We have stuff to drink here hon."

"Yes, that's it."

"All right, where is this to be delivered?"

Her shoulders dropped and she looked deflated. Laughing he gently took the phone from her and gave the person on the other end the address, then instructed them to call this number when they arrive and he'd walk out to the gate to get the order. When the person asked for form of payment, Shelby quickly jumped in, "I have cash."

Since it seemed important for her, he let her take charge of this, but he'd absolutely make it all up to her tomorrow.

Once that was out of the way, they settled in until their food arrived and he had never felt more fulfilled and happy then at this moment in his life.

If only things could stay just like this.

49

W ith their bellies full, the kids had fallen happily asleep on the sofa between them. Anders barely left Diego's lap so Diego leaned over to the side with his plate on the arm of the sofa to eat so he didn't drip on Ander's head. But he never complained. They talked about the movie a bit, they laughed at the funny parts and in the end, it had been a beautiful day. At least for the kids. Her heart was heavy, knowing she was keeping information from them, and also with the definitive truth that her beautiful sweet sister, Stacy, was never coming home. She'd had that feeling since Stacy first ended up missing, but now it was a fact and it hurt all over again.

Glancing over at Diego, their eyes locked. She whispered, "You're staring at me."

Nodding, he whispered back, "I love looking at you."

Her cheeks flushed and heated and a small smile played on his lips.

"Should we get these tired kiddos to bed?"

Without a word, he easily maneuvered a sleeping Anders into the crook of his arm while she managed to do the same with Callie.

"I'm tired." Callie sleepily said, though she wasn't fully awake.

"I know baby. Shh."

Diego stood once she had Callie and quietly walked to the bedroom, pulled the covers back and lay Anders on the queen bed on the left side while she mimicked his motions and lay Callie on the right side. Slowly covering them up and tucking them in, she kissed Callie's head then walked around the bed to kiss Anders. Before she passed Diego on the way to Anders, he pulled her into his arms and held her close for a few moments.

His hugs, gah, they were the best. She felt like super woman in his arms, like she could absorb his strength as he held her like this.

After holding her for a while, he kissed her lips softly, then smiled at her before walking to the foot of the bed to wait for her. Arranging the covers neatly over Anders, she leaned down and kissed his forehead, She straightened and Diego held his hand out to her. Hand in hand, they left together, quietly switching the light off and pulling the door to, but not latching it.

She began cleaning up the remnants of supper. Diego chuckled, "Do you want a beer or a glass of wine?"

"Ah, a beer sounds perfect right now."

He went to his room to grab the brews while she finished tidying, tossing the pizza and wings boxes into the garbage can by the door. Diego returned quickly and handed her a bottle. She happily took it, tapped her bottle to his and took a drink of the cold brew.

Immediately he kissed her lips softly, then pulled back and looked into her eyes.

"You're so good with them Shel."

"They're easy to be good to. I love them; they're good kids and I want only the best for them. That's why I did what I did and took them."

"I agree with you on all fronts and while, had we known each other before you took them, we'd have played this out differently, I'm glad they aren't in the hands of Kurtis any longer. Hopefully, they never will be again."

She turned to face him. "What are the chances of that happening? I mean, really happening?"

He shook his head. "I don't know. I've seen things go easy, and I've seen things go horribly awry. I don't want to predict and be wrong. But, I do know that between RAPTOR and GHOST, you've got the best of the best on your side and always remember you have an angel in heaven watching over you and wanting nothing more than for you to succeed. She did everything in her power to set that in motion."

She swallowed the sob that threatened to escape her throat and instead, inhaled a deep breath and held it for a few seconds before slowly releasing it.

"That's true. We have the most beautiful angel in heaven. Actually, we have two, my father is up there with Stacy too."

He leaned forward and kissed her forehead. "I'm sorry. I know that's hard."

Thinking a change in the subject would be best she looked into his handsome brown eyes. "What about your family, Diego. Are your parents alive? Do you have siblings?"

"My parents are still alive and live in Mississippi. They went there to work. I don't see them very often, but I call them once a week. I have one sister, Gabriella, and one brother, Daniel."

"Why do you and your sister have Hispanic names and Daniel does not?"

"My mother is Hispanic, my father Caucasian. Papa wanted Daniel named after his father. Mama wanted me named after hers."

She laughed. "That makes sense to me. Had Stacy and I been boys, we likely would have been named after our father and his father too. Instead, we were named because my mother liked our names." He chuckled and took a swig of his beer and she took a deep breath. "Did you ever marry?"

"Nope. When I was young all I wanted was to join the military and serve my country. You know, women love a man in uniform." He teased and she laughed.

"That's a fact."

"But, after serving two tours and my PTSD started up, I just didn't want to have to deal with it while entering a relationship. I had an opportunity to purchase a convenience mart so I did that thinking if I owned it and had the opportunity to set my own schedule and make my own rules, I wouldn't struggle so much with trying to keep a job if I had a bad night and wasn't able to cope during the following day. Or if I had an episode during the day and had to go somewhere until it passed. It didn't quite work out that way though. The stress of paying the bills, growing the business and the God-awful task of finding, training and dealing with employees who didn't give a shit made my PTSD worse. Therapy was expensive and time consuming and so I had almost given up. Then, Josh came to Texas and we all met up for our friend Travis' wedding and he had me working with him to find Isi's brother, Mateo. I realized I loved it. I missed that kind of work. And Josh got me in the program with Emmy and some of the others where I received the therapy I needed and the retraining I wanted. I've never been happier."

She wasn't sure how to take that.

50

D iego buttoned and zipped his black cargo pants —they were actually about all he owned. He did have a couple of pairs of dress pants, but these babies, well they worked. Sliding his belt through the loops, he then fastened it in the front and added his holster inside the waistband, tucked his wallet into his right back pocket and his cell phone into his left front pocket. He'd been excited all day to take Shelby out. This was the first real date he'd been on in years. Literally years. He'd removed himself from the dating world when he struggled with his PTSD and focused on his health, or rather, trying to find a way to be healthy. Then retraining and therapy took over and then RAPTOR happened. So, yeah. Years.

He dragged a brush through his hair and let it fall as it did before leaving. Life was pretty friggen good these days. And, now, Shelby and the kids. Yeah. Good.

Walking to Shelby's door he knocked once and heard her respond, "I'll be right there."

A few moments later she opened the door with a huge smile on her face. Her hair had a slight curl in it, and with the shorter cut, it added a bit of spunk to her appearance. She wore a touch of eye makeup and her lips shined and his heart roared to life. He'd always thought she was beautiful, but damn, right now she was a fucking knock-out.

"Wow, you look fantastic."

Her cheeks turned pink, which added to the beauty she already possessed and she looked down at the floor between them.

Reaching forward, he tucked his fingers under her chin and lifted her face to him. "You look gorgeous. You always do, I just wasn't expecting the makeup and hair. And it looks beautiful on you."

"Piper helped me with my hair, she even trimmed it in the back so it's even now. I hastily cut it on my own and haven't had a moment to get it fixed. She was sweet about helping me."

"Yeah. We have a great group here."

"They all like working with you too."

It was his turn to blush, a little bit anyway. "Thanks." Then he looked into her eyes. "I mean, thank you for telling me that. It's always nice to know."

She giggled and he liked it.

"Are you ready Shel?"

"Yeah. I just texted Isi. They're at Dodge and Jax's for dinner tonight and the kids are playing with the twins. Everyone is having fun."

"Great. So now you can relax a little bit and we can enjoy ourselves too."

He stepped aside and Shelby exited her room. Taking her hand in his, he pulled her to the elevator and waved his watch in front of the panel. The doors slid open with a swoosh and he held his hand out for Shelby to enter in front of him.

"So, I thought we'd go to the Copper Cup tonight and if there is somewhere else you prefer to go, just let me know. But they have great food and a pool table in the back where we can shoot a few games of pool."

"That sounds fun. I haven't shot pool in years."

"Don't tell me you're a shark."

She laughed and it looked fantastic on her. She seemed less stressed and more at ease tonight and he hoped he could keep it that way for her.

"No, I'm not a shark at all."

They walked through the garage to his truck and he helped her inside. Walking around the back of it, he climbed in the driver's side and started it up, stopping only to buckle his seatbelt. He backed from his space and put the truck in gear and left the garage.

Driving through town was peaceful and he managed to act the tour guide, at least as much as he could.

"So, that's the grocery store. In my opinion, that's where a lot of the gossip in town is spread. Those women who work the registers up front are absolutely gossip central."

She laughed and nodded. "Noted."

"So, it's your basic small town I guess. Bank, florist, bakery, hair salon, bars, gas stations, a couple of clothing stores, the works. But it's easy to navigate around, small enough where you get used to seeing the same cars in certain places and despite some of the issues it's had in recent years, it's relatively safe. Ford Montgomery and his son, Falcon, who works with me, grew up here. So, if you need a history lesson, one of them can fill you in."

"Okay. Wow, I didn't realize they were from here."

"Ford's sister is a prosecuter in town and his brother is a plumber."

She laughed again. "That's quite the varied experience."

He pulled into the lot behind the Copper Cup and put the truck in park. "This is the Copper Cup and our destination for the evening."

The back of the building was decorated with a large patio covered with a tin roof painted red, and colorful hanging baskets dangling all around the top of the rafters. It looked inviting.

"Do you know the owner of this place?"

"Yeah, Derek Thomas used to be the bartender, just bought it. He's a friend of Dodge's and a great guy."

They walked in the back door and a woman greeted them at the hostess stand.

"Hey there folks, inside or outside tonight?"

He looked at Shelby and she shrugged and smiled, "Outside sounds nice."

Winking at her he nodded, "Sounds good."

"Okay, then follow me please." She grabbed two menus and walked out the door they'd just entered through. Weaving between the tables, about half of them filled, she set them at the back corner table close to the railing. Perfect spot.

"Can I start you all off with a drink?"

He smiled at Shelby, waiting for her to order first. "I'll have a strawberry margarita."

"Sounds good. And for you sir?"

He chuckled. "I'll have a beer. Whatever you have on tap is great."

"Coming up."

She left the menus on the table and scooted off to get their drinks.

Opening her menu, Shelby asked, "What's your favorite item here?"

"I like the half rack of ribs and their cole slaw is the best I've ever had."

Shelby closed her menu and sat with her hands folded on top of it. "Sounds good to me."

He laughed then and reached across the table to hold her hand. When she turned her hand to link her fingers with his, his heartbeat sped up and he didn't want to stop looking at her. Captivating, he thought. She was captivating.

The waitress brought their drinks and took their orders and he raised his beer and tapped her glass. "Here's to life looking up."

"Cheers." She replied and took a drink of her margarita.

A car door slammed in the distance and kids playing in the yard across the road could be heard, birds chirped and it all seemed like the perfect summer evening.

"Tell me about your life before. What you did for a living. What you like doing in your free time," he asked.

She inhaled deeply. "I worked in a daycare. I also helped out in the office at the daycare with billing and other tasks, but mostly I enjoyed being with the kids. The pay wasn't the best, but I so loved spending time with the kids. They are innocent and joyful and some of them don't have great homes to go home to, so if I could give them some fun and love during the day to tide them over, I did that. I feel bad about how I left there, but I had no choice. Someday when this is all over, I'll call and apologize to them and hope they understand."

"I'm sure they will. These are extenuating circumstances."

She nodded and took a deep breath, then a sip of her drink. "I also like to garden in my spare time and I'm pretty good at canning and baking. Sort of boring, I know, but I had always dreamed I'd be a stay-at-home mom taking care of my family. All of that has been tossed out of the window now, but that's all I ever wanted."

"Was Stacy the same way?"

Shelby laughed. "Oh no. Stacy wanted to live like she was the star of that old show, Lifestyles of the Rich and

Famous. That was, until she got a real taste of what that meant."

Diego's phone rang and he pulled it from his front pocket. "Sorry."

"Josephs."

"Diego, it's Van, you have to get back here right away, it isn't safe for you and Shelby out there, Kurtis posted bond and is on the road and we think he's on his way here."

51

D iego stood, pulled money from his wallet and tossed it on the table, then took her hand while he walked them off the patio.

"How long since the last sighting?" he asked his caller.

Her heartbeat increased as she ran to keep up with his long strides. Fear clutched at her stomach and she wished she could hear who was on the other end of the phone so she knew what was going on.

He dropped her hand near the truck and pressed the fob through his pocket. He opened the passenger side and helped her climb up into his truck. Closing her door he hurriedly strode around the front of it and climbed into the driver's side. Diego turned the ignition and threw the truck into reverse. "We're on our way back. Keep me posted."

As they pulled out of the lot, he said, "Kurtis is on the loose and they think heading this way."

"How would he know where we are?"

"We must not have gotten to the trackers before he saw your location."

"Oh my God, the kids."

"They're in good hands. Van said he's alerting Josh, Dodge and Jax, so they'll be watching for any sign of Kurtis or anyone of his paid accomplices. I have to get you back to the compound for safety."

"I don't care about me, I only care about Callie and Anders," she wailed.

"I care about you," he snapped.

Her heart skipped a beat and she silently chastised herself for thinking life was on the mend.

Diego navigated the truck onto the main road, which was the only way to get back to the compound, and she kept scanning the area to make sure no one was hiding anywhere they passed.

Her throat closed up; she had a hard time swallowing and her breathing became uneven and choppy. She clasped her hands together as Diego watched the road carefully and glanced in his rearview mirror often.

Then she had a thought. "Oh my God, can he find the kids through their video games? They play online. Is that traceable?"

"Didn't they play when you were at the trailer?"

She thought for only a moment, "Yes, but not online, we didn't have internet there."

Diego glanced over at her and immediately tapped a button on his steering wheel. A phone began ringing through the speakers and Donovan answered.

"What'cha got?"

"Shelby just asked if the kids could be tracked through their video games. They play online with others."

"Hang on, let me check. I'll call you back. What's your ETA?"

"We're about ten minutes out."

"Roger."

The line went dead again and Diego glanced at her quickly. "That was some good thinking Shel. Thank you."

"What if it's too late. I never thought about that and I let them play online. They have a little group they play with and Stacy told me it was safe; she'd checked the kids out before allowing Callie and Anders to play with them. Some of the kids in that group are from their school."

"Don't think on the negative. Ever. We always have to think positive and look forward. Always."

Her hands fisted and for the first time ever, she doubted herself as the children's primary caretaker. She'd always thought she gave them all the love and support they needed. But, she stupidly realized she was ill-equipped to keep them safe.

Blinking rapidly to stem the flow of tears that threatened, she took a deep breath as Diego turned down the street the compound was located on.

Diego pushed a button on the dash of his truck and the gates opened up. He tapped another button and the garage doors opened, allowing them to pull right inside.

"Holy Fuck. Get down," he yelled.

She twisted to see what he was looking at but he pushed her head down as he shifted his truck into reverse and stomped on the gas. At the same time a cacophony of sounds rushed her ears. Glass breaking. Gun shots. The thud of something solid hitting the truck, or the other way around. Tires screeching and Diego yelling into his speakers. "Breach. Breach. Breach."

She hit the dash with her shoulder and tumbled off the seat to wedge herself between the dash and the seat as the truck stopped. As soon as the truck stopped completely Diego yelled, "Stay here. Stay down." He opened his door, pulled his gun out and walked to the back of the truck. She couldn't see him anymore.

Within seconds she could hear some of Diego's team members yelling, "Hands up." "I've got eyes." "Call an ambulance."

She took deep breaths trying to regain some semblance of control over her body. Inhale, hold for twelve seconds, exhale for twelve seconds. Repeat.

By her second deep breath more guns were fired and she screamed out at the surprise of the shots and held her breath as she waited to hear what happened. The silence was debilitating and she had to finally breathe again, so she slowly started her breathing once more. Thinking it was wise, she sent up a prayer to the good Lord to watch over those she loved and keep the children safe at all costs. He'd been looking over them so far.

Finally the passenger door opened and Diego's voice, so soft and reassuring called to her. "Shel, baby, let's get you out of here."

His gentle hands helped to pull her backwards as she tried unfolding herself from her bent position.

"Are you alright? I'm sorry I had to push you down. Did I hurt you?"

She opened her mouth to answer, but nothing came out so she shook her head quickly and turned her head to the left to see his worried, handsome face staring into hers.

Tears sprang to her eyes and she wrapped her arms around his shoulders as she jumped into his body, needing his strength and comfort. Just as quickly, she wondered if he needed hers too. His body shook slightly and in that split second she realized Ted was with the kids and not here to help Diego.

She kept her arms around his shoulders and softly spoke to him.

"Let's go sit down Diego. It's all good. We're all good."

She walked him into the garage and they sat on a bench just inside the door. He sat and she sat on his lap, hoping her weight would be similar to what Ted did for him. Wrapping her arms around his shoulders once again, she sat quietly holding him until she felt his body stop shaking. Soon after, his arms wrapped around her waist and his breathing evened out.

52

D iego inhaled deeply and let it out slowly.

"Thank you for helping me Shel."

She sobbed softly into his neck. "Oh my God, thank you for saving me."

"It was all I could think of at the time. Save Shelby."

"You did." Her voice broke and he squeezed her tightly and exhaled.

"Okay, so I don't know who the first man was, but he walked up behind us and had a gun pointed at your head through the back window. I hit him with the truck and then Kurtis came running up the driveway with a gun and one of my teammates shot him."

Another sob escaped her throat. "Is he dead?"

"I don't know yet."

"He's dead." Charly said as she entered the garage.

Shelby inhaled and nodded her head once. She turned to Charly. "Thank you."

Charly chuckled, "Sweetie, I wish I'd been the one but Van got that dirty dog. His accomplice is still alive and we have an ambulance on the way to take his ass to the hospital and the local PD coming to make sure he doesn't get out of the hospital."

Van came into the garage and walked toward them. His eyes landed on her briefly, then shifted to Diego.

"You good man?"

Diego nodded. "Yeah. Small episode, all good."

Van nodded. "I'll be tied up with PD for a while, just wanted to check before they get here."

Diego reached his hand out and shook Van's. "I'm sorry Van, but so fucking grateful. Thank you."

Van nodded again, then glanced at Charly before looking into Shelby's eyes. "We protect our own."

Tears sprang to Shelby's eyes at his kind words and what they meant. Charly then added, "Shelby, the kids are fine, I just got off the phone with Jax."

Shelby's hand flew to her mouth as she breathed through the emotion.

Diego pulled her tighter to him and she squeezed him with her arm around his shoulders. "I'll never be able to repay you all for what you've done for me."

Charly laughed, "Well, I've got some decorating that can be done."

Her eyes grew large and her eyebrows raised.

But Charly laughed again. "I've read your profile girl," she quipped and walked away.

Diego took a deep breath and exhaled slowly. "Are you okay? I need to go and see what's happening out there."

She rose from his lap; he stood and paused a moment before looking into her eyes. "Thank you for helping me," he whispered, a tad embarrassed by his episode.

She smiled as she returned his gaze. "Diego, honestly, thank you."

He kissed her lips softly then smiled. "I love you."

He was only slightly surprised that it flew from his mouth with such ease. He hadn't meant to declare his love, not so soon, but it seemed right.

Her bottom lip trembled as she stared at him, her face registering surprise. "I love you, too."

"I didn't really know it until your life was threatened. I knew I liked you. I liked being around you. I love the kids. But now I know, I love you, Shel."

She threw her arms around his shoulders and he pulled her into his arms until her feet left the floor. Diego chuckled. She giggled in return. It felt euphoric and exciting. This feeling had been absent from his life for so many years he'd thought it was lost to him forever.

Sirens grew louder as patrol cars sped to the driveway and suddenly ended their shrieking. "I need to go out there and we'll both need to make statements. But, you probably won't want to go out there until they put Kurtis in an ambulance."

"I'm fine and if you don't mind, I'd like to see him. I know it's morbid, but I want to know he will not be able to hurt the kids ever again."

He looked up and saw Emmy walking toward them. She smiled softly as she watched them and nodded when he looked up at her.

"Police are here Diego and you'll both need to make statements. Did you fire your weapon?"

"No. I pulled it but didn't fire it."

"Okay, Detective Rory Richards is here to speak with you."

He nodded and looked at Shelby. "Ready?"

"Yes."

Taking her hand, he walked them from the garage and toward Detective Richards. Reaching out to shake his hand, he nodded. "Rory, I'd like to introduce you to Shelby Davidson. Shelby, Rory and Ford are good friends and went to school together. He's lead detective here in Lynyrd Station and his wife, Alice, owns a detective agency in town, she's a hotshot PI."

Rory chuckled. "She's most certainly a hotshot. Nice to meet you Ms. Davidson. I'm sorry it's under these circumstances, though, and we'll need to interview you both individually."

Shelby smiled and he was proud of her strength. "I understand Detective. Who do you want to speak with first?"

"It doesn't matter. Why don't we start with you? Emmy said we could go to the conference room or we can stay out here on the front porch, which do you prefer?"

"Front porch is good."

She glanced up at him and smiled before walking to the porch with Rory and his heart swelled with pride. She was perfect for him.

An ambulance drove up the driveway toward him and he saw Shelby turn her head and look at Kurtis sprawled on the ground. EMT's quickly assessed his condition as deceased and loaded him on a gurney; as expected, he never moved. Shelby watched the whole thing; he understood her need to be sure. Kurtis had terrorized them all for so long and likely was the last person to see Stacy alive. Shelby had every right to ensure he would never do any of them harm again.

53

Sitting at the kitchen counter, Sheldon scooped a large helping of fresh baked apple pie onto her plate and set it in front of her.

He did the same for Diego then nodded. "Go on and eat. I don't want to hear you can't possibly, because my apple pie is the best in the land, I guarantee it."

Sheldon then busied himself with cleaning off the counter and putting away food containers. They'd come to the kitchen looking for a small snack after the police left because they'd not had anything since lunch. Sheldon was in working on his menu for the rest of the week and insisted they eat a full meal. Her stomach was close to bursting, but Sheldon had a kind but firm way of making meals mandatory and she didn't want him to be mad.

"Are you sure it's okay if the kids spend the night with Jax and Dodge?"

"Yes, you heard her, she's excited for them to stay. Maya and Myles love having them there and we'll go get them in the morning."

"Okay. I'll need to tell them everything tomorrow."

He locked eyes with her and nodded. "It's best. We'll both be here to spend time with them and make sure they're okay. We'll be able to answer questions and Isi will be here to in case they need any medical assistance."

She took a bit of pie and an involuntary "mmm" sounded from her throat. Sheldon stopped wiping the counter and smiled. "Told you."

After she'd finished the last bite of pie she pushed her plate away, "Sheldon, you'll have to stop force feeding me or I'll get big as a house."

He laughed. "Didn't see anyone forcing you, lady."

She laughed, too; well damn, he was right there.

Diego stood. "Thank you Sheldon, we appreciate you feeding us."

"That's what I do Diego and it's my pleasure. Good night folks."

Diego took her hand and they walked together from the kitchen through the dining room and to the elevator. Charly, Deacon and Falcon were in the living room talking when they walked past and they stopped at the doorway.

Diego asked, "Van get back yet?"

Falcon shook his head, "No, but he's on his way, we just got a text so we thought we'd wait for him in case he needs to decompress."

Diego nodded. "Thank you for that. We should wait too."

Charly laughed, "Get out of here. You both look like you're ready to fall over. After the pile of food Sheldon likely made you eat, you'll just be sleeping down here."

Shelby laughed, "That's a fact."

Diego waved. "Night folks."

Shelby waved too as they turned to leave amid the good nights from his co-workers and friends.

The ride upstairs was quiet but she was excited to be able to sleep with Diego tonight with the door locked.

He took the two steps to reach her and his hands dove into her hair as his lips touched hers. His were tentative at first, soft and molded perfectly to hers. Their kisses soon became urgent and demanding as his hands reached for her breasts. Soft kneading incited all delicious emotions in her and moisture gathered between her legs as the anticipation of being with Diego again grew inside of her.

Her hands sought his belt buckle and wrestled slightly with the clasp until she figured it out, all while continuing to kiss his lips. The button on his fly came next and then his zipper which, as soon as it was lowered, allowed her to slide her hands into his waistband and gently rub the length of his cock. The soft skin felt like the finest silk while the firmness beneath was a total turn on.

She wrapped her fingers around his length, and slowly pumped up and down. His breathing grew uneven and as he walked her backwards into the bedroom a thrill snaked through her body.

Once inside the bedroom he pulled his shirt over his head and let it fall to the floor. She wanted to touch him. Everywhere. And she proceeded to do just that. With one hand on his cock, her other hand smoothed over his warm firm chest and abs, the muscles beneath quivering at her touch.

Reluctantly he pulled back from her, shoved his pants down and stepped from them. His hands never missed a beat as they grabbed the bottom of her sweater to pull it over her head and toss it to the floor.

His fingers shook slightly as he unbuttoned her slacks; the zipper pulled down easily and he tugged them over her hips and let them fall to the floor.

She sat on the foot of the bed, intending to climb back, but his cock was right there in front of her face, so she took it in her hand and swiped her tongue over the top of it before sucking him into her mouth. His loud moan encouraged her as his hands dove into her hair, holding her head as his hips moved back and forth, aiding her mouth in taking him in.

His excitement fueled hers and grew with each stroke.

Suddenly he pulled away and gently pushed her to the bed. "Scoot back Shel."

She did as he commanded and he crawled back with her. Once her head was on the pillow, he hooked her right leg over his left arm, and slightly lifted her as he positioned himself at her entrance. She stretched her left leg out so she could feel him slide into her and it didn't disappoint. He moved slow and steady as he entered her, watching her face as he slid inside her body, every inch more exciting than the last. He slowly pulled out and thrust back in and the look in his gaze spoke volumes. He watched her with such intensity she knew he was memorizing this moment.

His hips swirled slightly and he hit her clit at the perfect angle. She moaned as the pleasure exploded through her. A small smile played on his lips, he'd been looking for that spot, so he hit it again and again and again. Her entire being focused in on the exquisite pressure drawing her closer to orgasm. Her body heated and her skin dampened as he continued to offer her pleasure; she gasped and clutched at his arms. Suddenly her orgasm raged through her like an inferno. Diego's eyes never left her as he watched as the ecstasy played over her face.

"That was beautiful," he husked out.

Then his hips moved faster as he neared his climax and she searched his face while his pleasure increased and finally exploded and she knew what he meant. It was beautiful.

54

He watched the kids closely as the day wore on. They'd cried when Shelby told them their mamma was now an angel. She was gentle with them, her voice so soothing, and Anders climbed in his lap and cried into his shoulder. He simply held Anders close and rubbed his hair and his back and told him he loved him and would always protect him.

Callie looked up at him after her tears had dried, her solemn eyes locked on his. He smiled softly at her, "I love you too, Callie. Your Aunt Shelby and I will always be here to protect you and keep you loved and happy. I promise."

Callie climbed into his lap next to Anders and he hugged her too. Shelby sat next to him on the floor rubbing Callie's back. "I love you both so much. But I also want you to know that I love Diego too."

Anders finally said, "I know."

He was so matter of fact about it they didn't even question that he did. Sometimes kids were more intuitive than adults gave them credit for.

After some time together in their room, Callie asked if they could go outside and play and Shelby and he thought that was a good sign.

So, they were now outside in the yard watching the kids chase butterflies, their giggles coming back to them. Emmy found a rubber ball in the workout room and they kicked that around a bit too. They needed to be tired out. Axel and Bridget brought Aidyn over a couple of hours ago and they worked together on a science project. They each found a cocoon in the bushes; Axel cut the branches the cocoons were on and they each had a glass jar provided by Sheldon to put their cocoons into. Each day they were supposed to watch it and one day it would emerge a butterfly.

He looked over at the GHOST compound and pulled Shelby close to him. "You know, Jax and Josh planted a tree over there for their father and one for their brother Jake. Dodge planted a tree alongside for his son Adam. We could plant a tree here for Stacy and the kids can take care of it and watch it grow."

The look on her beautiful face when she looked up at him was breath taking. "Oh, Diego, what a beautiful idea. Oh, do you think we can do that?"

"I don't see why not."

"But, what happens now? We can't stay here. I mean, won't Emmy want us to leave now?"

"When I met you things were upside down. I thought you were bad and I had to bring you in. It didn't take me long to figure out that things weren't what they seemed. From that moment on I was falling in love with you. With all of you. Does that make sense? All my life I was just me, alone against the world sort of. I felt damaged and out of control of my own body, never knowing when I'd have an episode or if I would. Ted helped of course. But, I didn't think I'd get to have a family of my own. I also didn't think I was missing anything in not having that. I just thought that was what my life would be. But you all have changed me and what I want for my future. I want you all in my life every day. I want to wake up every morning to you and the kids and Ted. I want to hear you laugh and the kids' giggles and messy breakfasts and dirty clothes, skinned knees and sports games and homework and most of all, love. I love you all so much."

Diego paused and looked into her eyes, "Marry me, Shelby. Be my wife. I'll adopt the children, we'll adopt the children and be a family. We can stay here or if you want we can move to our own little house. We'll plant a tree here and one wherever we end up living later if we move."

As she processed what he'd asked, her eyes glistened with unshed tears and her bottom lip quivered. "I love you Diego." A tear slid down her cheek, "Yes." She wrapped her arms around his shoulders. "Yes, I want all of that too."

He kissed her lips; they still quivered from her surprise, but he enjoyed the feel of her lips against his. When he pulled back, he laughed and picked her up and spun her around. She pressed into his neck as she held on to him and when he set her down, he kissed her lips again.

Callie giggled and Anders sounded disgusted when he said, "Gross."

Diego and Shelby both laughed. He knelt down and looked them both in the eyes.

"I just asked Aunt Shelby to marry me. We can be a family if you agree. Would you both agree that Aunt Shelby and I marry and we can adopt you and be a family forever."

Anders started crying and walked into his arms and Diego's heart felt like it would break. It was likely too much for him all in one day. He wrapped both of his arms around Anders and held him tight, trying to push all of his love into this sweet little boy. He glanced at Callie who stood watching them and he opened his arms to her too. She tentatively walked to him and he wrapped her and Anders into a hug.

Shelby scooted close and whispered, "Family hug." And Diego's arm snaked out and wrapped her up with them. They hugged for a long moment until the kids felt ready to step away and Diego smiled at Callie and Anders. "Was that a yes?"

Callie looked into Shelby's eyes, "I want to live with you both and be a family."

Anders nodded then in true Anders style said, "Can I get a new video game?"

55

S helby wiped the counter off and put the milk in the refrigerator. Tomorrow was the final proceeding in the Estate of both Kurtis and Stacy Kennedy. Because of the convoluted mess Kurtis had created, the courts first had to decide that he'd been guilty of killing Stacy. Which it had decided last month. The evidence had been sufficient that he'd pushed her down the stairs, with both the kids having to tell this to a social worker in separate interviews and the fact that the same evening, the neighbor's doorbell camera caught Kurtis driving away around 10:30 and not returning until 2:15 the next morning. Piecing this all together, that was enough time for him to drive the many miles to toss her suitcase, a few more miles to dispose of her body and then get back to the house. The police had also determined that Kurtis was blackmailing politicians, which to Shelby's irritation, never made the news, largely because the political party at fault controlled the media, thereby quashing any negative mention of the guilty politicians who'd had sex with underage girls and who needed to be brought to justice.

Diego promised her that RAPTOR would continue Stacy's work on that front.

The man that Kurtis had brought to RAPTOR to kill her survived and filled in the missing details, allowing police to fully piece the complete story together. Detective Richards had helped the Kansas City Police and between both departments, the Court said there was no hesitancy in its decision to name Kurtis as Stacy's murderer, thereby also pulling his fortune from his awful family, who had suddenly come out of the woodwork with their hands out, wanting money and the house and to run the company. His whole family was rotten to the core. She'd also vowed that Callie and Anders would never have anything to do with any of them.

Tomorrow, they hoped and prayed and expected the Judge to rule that Callie and Anders were the sole heirs, and therefore, the full beneficiaries of the Kennedy estate. She also hoped that the Judge would name her as the guardian and grant her and Diego permission to adopt the children.

Turning off the kitchen light, she walked into the living room where Diego sat reading one of his books. He looked peaceful, his feet raised in his recliner, his face in rest, his eyes scanning the pages of the paperback he held. She'd thought right away he was sexy, but a man who reads, now damn, that is hella sexy.

Diego looked up at her and smiled, "What are you looking at?"

She giggled and sat in the recliner next to him, "I think you're sexy and I love looking at you."

Leaning over he kissed her lips, then smiled. "The kids fell asleep fast."

"They did. Skye Winters did their lessons today and they did art class. She had them scouring the yard for pretty stones in the landscaping, straight sticks from the trees and pretty leaves. It wore them out. I'd bet Maya, Myles, Aiden and Tate are sleeping soundly too. And, they love their new bunk beds."

He chuckled, "I don't know how she keeps those littlest ones busy while trying to keep the older ones in learning mode. In another year, Hawk and Roxanne's little guy will be joining the mix."

"She manages. It's impressive to watch. I have them all on Thursday and we're supposed to do some sort of cooking class. I asked Sheldon to help me. We're making mini-cupcakes and making it a math lesson too."

Diego laughed out loud, "Oh, I hope I'm around to watch that. Sheldon is very specific about his kitchen."

She laughed with him. It would be interesting for certain. She inhaled deeply and let out her breath slowly and Diego reached over and took her hand in his.

"Don't be nervous; tomorrow is the final hearing and even Attorney Wingert said it's a formality. After tomorrow, we'll be able to plan our wedding and work with Attorney Wingert on selling the big house and selling off SmartTech."

She looked into his sexy brown eyes. "I know, I just always worry his family will try to pull something."

Nodding, Diego replied, "They can try, but they'll get nowhere. The Judge has already told them the only way for them to get the company is to buy it. None of them have the money, and if they can find it, fine, all that matters is the kids get the money to put in their trust accounts." He turned slightly to face her, "And that the software that Kurtis had inserted into the kids video games online, never see the light of day to track anyone else in that way.

"Yeah." She turned to look at the kitchen.

Emmy had given them permission to knock the wall out between Diego's apartment and the one she and the kids shared. Since they didn't need two living rooms, they added a small kitchen in the former living room of her apartment, which made snack time and early mornings when the kids woke much easier for them to manage. They still ate most of their meals with the rest of the crew and she'd grown to love it. The kids did too. They were thriving here. So many adults for them to count on, other kids next door at GHOST and associated with them, to play with and the kids were all homeschooled by them. Bridget, Skye, Sophie, Bridget's mom, Vivian, and Jax's mom, Pilar. Everyone brought a different perspective to learning. With them all as a team, the kids were well-rounded and happy.

"Hey." Diego took her hand. "What's going on in your head?"

She turned in her seat to face him. "Once the big house sells, what do you want to do? Do you want to stay here or move to our own house?"

Setting his book on the table beside him, he turned to her, "What do you want to do?"

She laughed, "I asked you first."

He looked thoughtful for a while then he smiled sweetly. "I'd like to stay here. We have such strong support for the kids here. It's only been seven months since you came here and moving them away from all of these folks they love might make it hard for them to handle on top of all the other changes."

She nodded. He continued, "But, if you're unhappy here, we can find a place close by and move."

Shaking her head, she stopped him. "No, I've grown to love it here. I just worried you'd want to leave."

"Why? Everything I love is here. It's easy for work and if I have to be on a mission, I know you and the kids are safe, protected, and have people here to lean on if things get hard."

She smiled and lay her hand on the side of his face, her thumb roving over his cheek. "I love you Diego and we'll go anywhere you go."

He stood and reached down to pick her up. She quickly wrapped her legs around his waist and he nuzzled her neck. "Good, why don't we go to bed then, and you can show me how much you love me. Then, the instant we walk out of court tomorrow, we'll plan in earnest for our wedding. We've put it off for too long. I want to officially be a family."

She giggled as she nibbled on his neck, "Sounds perfect."

56

The Bailiff called, "All rise."

They rose as the Judge entered the courtroom. He took Shelby's hand in his, his thumb absently playing with the engagement ring he and the kids picked out for her. He smiled every time he saw her looking at it, but he couldn't wait to add the wedding band to it. Waiting for these court dates to be over so they could move on with their lives had felt like living in a small jail cell. They wanted to move forward, but they needed to wait until all of this was behind them. They had decided on a family vacation together instead of a honeymoon. The kids wanted to go to Disney so that's where they were headed. In a couple of months.

Shelby had her dress, he had a suit, their attendants were chosen, Josh for him and Shelby had asked Charly to be her maid of honor. Charly was so excited she squealed. They weren't going to have any others, they wanted everyone to feel included.

The Judge situated himself on his chair and looked over to the opposite side of the courtroom where he, Shelby, and her attorney, Spencer Wingert, sat, to where Kurtis Kennedy's brother, Kevin, and his team of attorneys sat. They'd argued earlier that the brother should get the company, SmartTech, for some nonsensical reason, which the Judge seemed bored to tears with.

When the brother then asked for custody of the children, the Judge shut them right down. "Mrs. Kennedy, knew your brother was of dubious character, some of which you've mirrored here yourself Mr. Kennedy, and she had proper papers drawn up asking that her sister be the legal guardian of the children. I see no reason why I wouldn't grant that permission."

"Your honor..."

"I won't entertain any more of your whimsical arguments. I am now ready to rule."

The Judge looked at Shelby, "You've shown that you value those children more than your own life and your sister was wise to name you as their guardian. I therefore grant full custody of Callie Kennedy and Anders Kennedy to you, Shelby Davidson, and therefore encourage you and your fiancé, Diego Josephs, to proceed with adoption as soon as you are married."

"Your Honor, with all due respect..."

"Mr. Kennedy, you will not disrespect the court. Mr. Whilen, you will keep your client calm or he will be escorted from the court."

"Yes your Honor."

"Further," the Judge continued, "SmartTech will be placed in the hands of Ms. Davidson, whom I understand has a trustee to manage it for her and the children, to run or sell or whatever she decides."

Diego glanced over at Kevin Kennedy and saw him jawing away at his attorney, though quietly. He squeezed Shelby's hand and she swiped at a tear that had trailed down her cheek.

"Finally, Ms. Davidson, you may either live in the Kennedy house or dispose of it at your will, it is the property of the children and therefore as their guardian, yours to manage how you see fit. I'll also add, if you are given any sort of trouble during the disposal of any of the property, the company or any of the personal property items, I order that you only need to call the police and they will have a standing order to arrest anyone interfering with yours and the children's rights to any of the property."

Shelby nodded at the judge, though the tears were still falling. "Thank you your Honor."

With that, the Judge tapped his gavel on the disk and stood to exit the court.

Shelby turned to him and he held her close, "Congratulations Shel, it's all over now. Mostly."

He reached forward and shook Attorney Wingert's hand. "Thank you for all of your hard work Attorney Wingert."

"Spencer, please. You're welcome, both of you. This was as much a pleasure to ensure those depraved people didn't get anything from the children, as it was a job."

Shelby smiled and hugged Attorney Wingert. "Thank you. My sister did a beautiful job of selecting the appropriate attorney to hold her secrets and carry out her wishes."

Attorney Wingert choked up at her praise and nodded. "I'd say your sister was a fine judge of character. She chose the best for her children as well."

He turned to see daggers being shot from across the room at them and he softly said, "Let's wait for them to get out of here before we have to go out."

Spencer Wingert responded, "It would be stupid of them to try anything here under the watchful eyes of the Judge and all the police officers milling about. But, it would also help you if they did to solidify the judge's order in the minds of all who questioned it."

Shelby nodded. "Well the first order of business is to fire Kevin Kennedy from SmartTech. He'll do nothing but cause problems there now to diminish the value of the company. So, Spencer, can you please make sure the Trustee handles that immediately? I don't even want him going inside today. If that means a police presence out front, so be it. It will also entail security accesses being denied and if he has people on the inside, they need to be removed from the property as well."

Diego laughed, "You're a ruthless business woman Shelby. I'm proud of you."

Attorney Wingert smiled at Shelby, "Done and done. Also, I'll begin negotiating with the interested buyer I mentioned yesterday."

Shelby nodded, "Yes, please. The sooner the better."

Kevin Kennedy left the courtroom and they waited only a couple of minutes to exit. As they walked out to the atrium in the courthouse, Kevin Kennedy rushed over yelling, "How dare you fire me and cut off access to my phone, credit cards and security clearance."

Shelby straightened her shoulders and looked him square in the eye. "How dare you act righteous and indignant. Your brother was a crook, a liar, a cheater, a blackmailer and a murderer. You and your family have done enough to sully your name and that of the company and to harm the children. There will be no more opportunities for you to cause them any harm and having you in any proximity to the company or to them, is potential to cause them harm."

He stared at her, his attorney trying to calm him down, clearly nervous about the ramifications of creating a scene here or anywhere. Shelby stared at him as long as he stared at her. Then she stared a bit longer, effectively winning the stand-off. Once Kevin turned and stomped away, she slowly let out a breath, then her shoulders relaxed.

Diego leaned into her, placed his arm around her shoulders and kissed her temple. "Badass right there Shel."

"I'm just so sick of that family. They're all nothing but trash. Not once did any of them show disgust to Kurtis' actions. Not once did any of them mention the fact that he murdered Stacy. They can all rot as far as I'm concerned."

Diego smiled. "I'm so proud of you. Let's go home and plan a wedding and an adoption."

After parking in the garage, he jumped out of the truck and walked around the passenger side to open Shelby's door. He held his hand out and helped her down then leaned in and kissed her lips.

"I love you Shel."

She smiled up at him, "I love you too Diego. What do you think of getting married next week?"

"I'd say why do we have to wait a week."

She laughed and he laughed too. It felt good. He took her hand as they walked to the elevator and she stopped. "I was serious. Showing the kids this is all over with and moving on with us as a family is what we all want. I don't need a big fancy to do. Rather than having us all feeling like we're waiting for other events to take place to move on, let's just do it. Get married and immediately file the adoption papers with the court. Our honeymoon and family vacation can wait until we make the adoption final. That will be our first real family outing. What do you say?"

He pulled her in for a hug and enjoyed the way she felt against his body. "You had me at getting married next week."

The elevator doors opened and Van and Charly stepped out.

"Hey, how did court go?" Charly asked.

Shelby responded, "Perfect. It's all over."

Charly hugged Shelby then stepped back. "So when are you getting married?"

Shelby laughed. "Next week."

"Oh my gosh, that's awesome. Okay, well, Van and I are heading out to do some surveillance. But when I get back, let's talk about what has to be done."

Diego looked at Van. "What's up?"

"I think I got a location on Marco48. I want to go see the location to see if I'm right."

"That's fantastic. I'm back at it so call if you need assistance."

"Got it. Glad everything worked out for you Shelby."

Van and Charly walked to Van's SUV and Diego held the elevator doors for Shelby. Once inside she asked, "Who's Marco48?"

"He's a pedophile Van has made contact with on the internet. Van is pretending to be a young boy looking for a hookup."

"Oh my God, that is so sick."

"It's what we do Shel. We need to stop these assholes."

"I'm sending positive thoughts to Van and Charly and hope Marco48 goes down hard."

***

Diego and Shelby's story isn't finished yet, you are cordially invited to the wedding - Diego and Shelby's Wedding

If you're reading this in paperback form, use this link - https://dl.bookfunnel.com/dm9dt7lp8v

As you can tell, Donovan is about to get into something deep. Keep reading to see what he has going. Or, if you prefer, grab your copy of Holding Hadleigh and watch the sparks fly. https://www.pjfiala.com/books/HH-Amazon

Keep in touch and learn about new releases, sales, recipes, and other fun things by signing up for my newsletter - https://www.subscribepage.com/PJsReadersClub_copy

ALSO BY PJ FIALA

Click here to see a list of all of my books with the blurbs.

Contemporary Romance

Rolling Thunder Series

Moving to Love, Book 1

Moving to Hope, Book 2

Moving to Forever, Book 3

Moving to Desire, Book 4

Moving to You, Book 5

Moving Home, Book 6

Moving On, Book 7

Rolling Thunder Boxset, Books 1-4

Military Romantic Suspense

Second Chances Series

Designing Samantha's Love, Book 1

Securing Kiera's Love, Book 2

Second Chances Boxset - Duet

Bluegrass Security Series

Heart Thief, Book One

Finish Line, Book Two

Lethal Love, Book Three

Bluegrass Security Boxset, Books 1-3

Big 3 Security

Ford: Finding His Fire Book One

Lincoln: Finding His Mark Book Two

Dodge: Finding His Jewel Book Three

Rory: Finding His Match Book Four

Big 3 Security Boxset, Books 1-4

GHOST

Defending Keirnan, GHOST Book One

Defending Sophie, GHOST Book Two

Defending Roxanne, GHOST Book Three

Defending Yvette, GHOST Book Four

Defending Bridget, GHOST Book Five

Defending Isabella, GHOST Book Six

RAPTOR

RAPTOR Rising - Prequel

Saving Shelby, RAPTOR Book One

Holding Hadleigh, RAPTOR Book Two

Craving Charlesia, RAPTOR Book Three

Promising Piper, RAPTOR Book Four

Missing Mia, RAPTOR Book Five

Believing Becca, RAPTOR Book Six

Keeping Kori, RAPTOR Book Seven

Healing Hope, RAPTOR Book Eight

Engaging Emersyn, RAPTOR Book Nine

MEET PJ

Writing has been a desire my whole life. Once I found the courage to write, life changed for me in the most profound way. Bringing stories to readers that I'd enjoy reading and creating characters that are flawed, but lovable is such a joy.

When not writing, I'm with my family doing something fun. My husband, Gene, and I are bikers and enjoy riding to new locations, meeting new people and generally enjoying this fabulous country we live in.

I come from a family of veterans. My grandfather, father, brother, two sons, and one daughter-in-law are all veterans. Needless to say, I am proud to be an American and proud of the service my amazing family has given.

My online home is https://www.pjfiala.com.
You can connect with me on Facebook at https://www.facebook.com/PJFiala1,

and
Instagram at https://www.Instagram.com/PJFiala.
If you prefer to email, go ahead, I'll respond -
pjfiala@pjfiala.com.

Made in the USA
Monee, IL
23 September 2022